KU-654-997

HELL'S COURTYARD

Indian Territory, popularly called Hell's Courtyard, was where bad men fled to escape the law. Buck Rogan, a deputy marshal hunting the killer Jed Calder, found the trail leading into Hell's Courtyard and went after his quarry, finding every man's hand against him. Rogan was also searching for the hideout of Jake Yaris, an outlaw running most of the lawlessness directed at Kansas and Arkansas. Single-minded and capable, Rogan would fight the bad men to the last desperate shot.

Books by Corba Sunman
in the Linford Western Library:

RANGE WOLVES
LONE HAND
GUN TALK
TRIGGER LAW
GUNSMOKE JUSTICE
BIG TROUBLE
GUN PERIL
SHOWDOWN AT SINGING SPRINGS
TWISTED TRAIL
RAVEN'S FEUD
FACES IN THE DUST
MARSHAL LAW
ARIZONA SHOWDOWN
THE LONG TRAIL
SHOOT-OUT AT OWL CREEK
RUNNING CROOKED

CORBA SUNMAN

HELL'S COURTYARD

Complete and Unabridged

LINFORD
Leicester

Northamptonshire
Libraries

E

First published in Great Britain in 2008 by
Robert Hale Limited
London

First Linford Edition
published 2009
by arrangement with
Robert Hale Limited
London

The moral right of the author has been asserted

Copyright © 2008 by Corba Sunman
All rights reserved

British Library CIP Data

Sunman, Corba.
    Hell's Courtyard
    1. Western stories.
    2. Large type books.
    I. Title
    823.9'14–dc22

    ISBN 978–1–84782–625–1

Published by
F. A. Thorpe (Publishing)
Anstey, Leicestershire

Set by Words & Graphics Ltd.
Anstey, Leicestershire
Printed and bound in Great Britain by
T. J. International Ltd., Padstow, Cornwall

This book is printed on acid-free paper

1

Buck Rogan emerged from the hills overlooking Fort Bradnum, West Arkansas, and reined in to check the hoofprints of the killer, Jed Calder, which he had followed south from Kansas into Indian Territory — the haunt of many criminals running from the law. Calder had murdered an influential rancher, Ben Harmon, and his family, on the range south of Dodge City. Rogan, a deputy US marshal, worked out of Topeka under the auspices of the governor of Kansas. He had been sent to hunt down the cold-blooded slayer with orders to take him dead or alive, and further, he was instructed to follow up the rumour that a great number of badmen were operating out of Indian Territory from a robbers' roost organized by Jake Yaris, the notorious leader of one of the biggest outlaw gangs in the West.

Rogan had twice brushed with Calder since leaving Kansas but sheer bad luck had prevented a capture. Jed Calder was a small man with murderous tendencies, and the twin .45 pistols he carried in sagging cartridge belts around his waist made him a tough proposition for any lawman. Calder's trail had led into the territory of Oklahoma before passing into the Hell's Courtyard of Indian Territory and then angling east into Arkansas. All Rogan could do was stick to the tenuous trail until the killer finally decided to stop running. During his wide-ranging hunt for Calder, Rogan had heard many rumours about Jake Yaris and the alleged big hideout, and was impatient to get on the trail of the outlaws.

Aware that he was down to his last dollar, Rogan checked Calder's tracks and noted that they headed straight into Fort Bradnum. He was about twenty-four hours behind the killer, and needed to get into town before the bank closed. He touched spurs to his bay and pushed on down a long incline to the distant main street, aware that Calder could not run for ever.

Rogan was a big man, two inches over six feet in height, wide-shouldered and powerful, with not an ounce of extra flesh on his frame. His face was angular and not unhandsome, with flat planes to his cheeks and a thin-lipped mouth adorned by a thick black moustache. His dark eyes were filled with an alertness that came from the hazardous job he had followed with great success for the past four years, before which he had been a deputy town marshal for two years at Dodge City. His habitual expression of remoteness mingled with hardness carried a tacit warning to all who encountered him that he was a man not to be discounted in any situation.

It was just after noon when he entered Fort Bradnum. He reined up at the entrance to the wide main street and studied details. His clothes were dusty and trail-worn — denim pants, a dark shirt, drab vest, and a short leather jacket. His narrowed brown eyes were shaded by the wide brim of his black Stetson, and they missed nothing along the street. He was wearing a leather cartridge belt with the holster, in which nestled a Colt .45 Peacemaker, tied down on his right thigh.

Rogan spotted the bank down on the right just before the law office. His first thought was for the care of his horse, but he needed money urgently and rode past Goymer's livery barn to dismount in front of the bank. He wrapped his reins around a hitching rail fronting the brick building beside three other horses and stepped up on to the wooden sidewalk. He paused to check the street again, but failed to see anyone who resembled Jed Calder amongst the inevitable idlers.

Rogan pushed open the door of the bank, walked into the gloomy interior, and froze into immobility when a pistol muzzle jabbed against his spine as he was closing the door. A hand snatched his .45 from its holster and a harsh voice snarled in his ear.

'Stand mighty still, mister, and don't do anything with your hands. If you want some dough from this place then you're outa luck. We're taking the lot. Get over there by the far wall and lie down on your belly. I'll put a slug through you if you so much as blink.'

Rogan heard the clatter of his pistol being thrown into a corner as he obeyed the command. He got down on his belly, his hands spread out on the floor above his head, and did not move a muscle. From the sound of the harsh voices of the robbers he surmised there were three of them at work, and recalled the three horses standing beside his own animal at the hitching rail out front. A timeless period ensued, and then one of the robbers spoke sharply.

'We're leaving now, and anybody who sticks his nose outside the door inside of five minutes will get it blown off.'

The street door was opened and boots thudded on the bare boards. Rogan lifted his head, saw that the robbers had departed, and sprang to his feet. He ran across to the corner where his gun had been tossed and snatched it up. Outside, the clatter of a trio of horses leaving in a hurry indicated that the robbers were making their getaway. Rogan ran out to the sidewalk.

The robbers were fifty yards away and moving fast. One of them was peering back over his shoulder, looking for resistance, and raised a pistol to start shooting. His first bullet struck a lantern on the wall beside the bank. Rogan lifted his pistol and worked the trigger. Gun smoke flared and crashing shots blasted through the silence. His first shot struck the nearest of the crooked trio, and the man was still falling out of his saddle when Rogan's second bullet smacked into the spine of the second robber, who pitched lifelessly into the dust, the loaded saddlebags on his shoulder rolling on the hard ground.

The third robber swung left into a narrow alley and disappeared from sight even as Rogan drew a bead on him. Rogan paused, breathing through his open mouth, and listened to the sullen echoes of the quick shots fading across the town. A few tense moments passed before animation returned to the shocked townsfolk who had inadvertently witnessed the shooting.

Rogan broke his pistol and reloaded the spent chambers. The door of the bank stood wide open and a big man dressed in a brown store suit appeared in the entrance, his ageing face ghastly white with shock. His hands were trembling when he paused at Rogan's side and gazed silently at the two sprawled bodies along the street.

'You'd best pick up those saddlebags before someone else runs off with them,' Rogan said quietly. The man nodded and drew a deep breath before hurrying off along the street.

'What happened here?' a voice demanded behind Rogan, who turned to see a man wearing a town marshal's law star on his shirt front emerging from the law office next to the bank.

'Frank Halfnight!' Rogan ejaculated.

'Buck Rogan!' the town marshal responded, and came forward with outstretched hand. 'What brings you into our neck of the woods, Buck? I heard you were working out of the governor's office in Topeka, and doing a great job.'

'I'm hunting a killer name of Jed Calder. His tracks led me here.'

'You think he's in town? We'll get together on that in a moment. Were you involved in the shooting here?'

Rogan recounted the incident and they walked towards the two slumped bodies in the street.

'So this is where you ended up after leaving Dodge City,' Rogan observed. 'You had a big dream in your mind back then, Frank. You were gonna do big things. What happened to bring you here?'

'A woman is back of it but she is long gone, Buck.' Halfnight sighed. He was tall and lean, with blue eyes and light-brown hair. He smiled ruefully. 'So much for my big plans, huh? All I've managed to do is finish up on the edge of Hell's Courtyard out here in the back of beyond. I would have done better had I stayed in Dodge. At least there was more life in the city. Here it's just a boring round of being ready for the badmen sneaking east out of Indian Territory.'

'You must remember that the same thing happens in Kansas,' Rogan reminded. 'We get a lot of badmen coming up from the Territory, stealing and murdering before heading back to the safety of wherever they hide out. I've heard that somewhere in the wilderness there's a big hideout run by Jake Yaris, with mebbe fifty badmen using it as a refuge. Most of the raids in Kansas and Arkansas are hatched out in that Devil's Nest.'

Halfnight laughed and shook his

head. 'Sure, and I've heard of El Dorado to the south, but no one's found that cache of gold yet, and if you wander into Indian Territory looking for that hideout and the bunch that's supposed to use it then you might never ride out again. There is a hardcase by the name of Jake Yaris, but nobody knows where he's at.'

'From what I've heard about him I'd say it's more than a rumour,' Rogan persisted.

'You could be right, Buck, and I reckon the best thing you can do is ride to Fort Smith and have a talk with Judge Parker. He's running all the law operations against the badmen in Indian Territory, and they do say he's making a real good job of it.'

They reached the nearer of the two robbers. Halfnight bent over the dead man and turned him face upward. He grinned admiringly and shook his head in disbelief.

'You ain't lost your edge yet, Buck' he observed. 'Shot him off a running horse at fifty yards and hit him plumb between the shoulder blades. Let's take a look at the other one.'

'Do you know this one?' Rogan asked.

Halfnight shook his head. 'Nope. He's just another of the multitude of thieves we're plagued with. There must be several hundred of them hiding out in Indian Territory, although I don't think they're as organized as you think they might be. They just lie low out there until they need more dough and head in this direction or go north into Kansas. We don't seem to be making much headway against them, and by the sound of it you aren't making an impact on them either, but Judge Parker over in Fort Smith has got the right idea. They don't call him the 'Hanging Judge' for nothing. He's got Bill Tilghman and Heck Thomas working for him, and they've recruited close to two hundred deputies in groups of four and five to ride into Indian Territory and flush out the badmen.'

'That's good news,' Rogan commented. 'I've heard of the judge.'

'They do say Parker has hanged more than fifty men since he started operating. Now if you talked with him and persuaded him to send all his deputies in a bunch to look for that hideout — if there is one, then you might succeed in smashing the hold the badmen have over us.'

'That sounds like a good idea. I reckon it's the only way to beat lawlessness. When I've handled Calder I might take a ride over to Fort Smith.'

Halfnight dropped to one knee beside the second dead man. 'I know this face,' he said. 'It's Walt Gauvin, a two-bit rustler and robber. He sure tried for the big time, coming into town to rob the bank, and was mighty unlucky to run into you, huh? But they all get their come-uppance in the end.'

'The third robber rode into that alley on the left,' Rogan said. 'I reckon he'll be halfway to Fort Smith by now.'

'He's more likely to be heading back

into Hell's Courtyard,' Halfnight observed.

'Back to the big hideout, huh?' Rogan smiled.

'I'll get a posse out after him.' Halfnight turned to the man who had retrieved the stolen money and who was standing nearby, motionless in shock, and clutching the saddlebags to his chest. 'You better get back inside the bank with that dough, Charles,' he advised. 'It was lucky for you Buck Rogan was in the right place at the right time. Buck, this is Charles Harper, the banker.'

'I'm mighty thankful for your intervention, sir,' Harper, a tall, heavy man in his fifties, spoke quickly. 'I feared for your life when you entered the bank while the robbery was in progress. Thank heaven you did exactly what you were told.'

'I came into the bank because I need some spending money,' Rogan said. 'I'm down to my last dollar.'

'Come and see me when you're through out here,' Harper replied warmly. He turned and hurried back along the street.

'There goes one mighty relieved man,' Halfnight observed. He scanned the faces of the dozen or so townsfolk who were converging on the two dead men. 'Pete, fetch Redfern to take care of these stiffs. Benson, call out three or four of the regular possemen and see if you can pick up that third robber. He rode into Coe's Alley.'

The two men departed, and Halfnight beckoned a small, thin man who was standing on the edge of the gathering crowd.

'Hey, John,' he called. 'There are a couple of saddle horses along the street. Pick them up and keep them in your barn until I can get around to them.'

'Sure thing, Frank!' The liveryman turned away.

'That's John Cahill,' Halfnight informed Rogan. 'If you can describe the horse your killer is riding then Cahill is the man to talk to.'

Halfnight called Cahill and the

liveryman paused.

'This is Buck Rogan, US Deputy Marshal,' Halfnight introduced. 'John Cahill, Buck.'

'A killer has ridden into town,' Rogan said. 'He was riding a big chestnut horse that's got a lot of white on its back legs. I reckon he would try to swap that horse for a fresh animal, and you're most likely to have seen him.'

'I've got the horse you describe in my barn right now,' Cahill said.

'Can you describe the man who left it?' Rogan asked.

'What did your killer look like?' Cahill countered.

'He's a small man with a leering grin on his face and teeth which remind you of a pack-rat. His expression never changes. I reckon he'll be wearing that grin when he finally crosses the Great Divide. He carries twin pistols on crossed cartridge belts, and doesn't seem big enough to handle them, but he's deadly — has a string of killings to his name.'

'I've seen him.' Cahill nodded. 'I didn't like the look of him, but he did a straight swap for one of my horses, and seemed to be in a real hurry to shake the dust of the town off his feet. He rode out fast about noon and headed straight into Indian Territory — Hell's Courtyard, they call it, and they sure got that right. Come along to the stable when you got time and we'll talk about your man.'

Rogan nodded. 'I need to go into the bank. Then I'll come and see you.'

Cahill departed. Rogan turned back to the bank, wanting to get his business settled and be on his way. Halfnight walked with him to the door of the bank and paused. He held out his hand and Rogan clasped it warmly, then watched as Halfnight departed to attend his duties. Rogan entered the bank and withdrew twenty dollars from a special expense account. He went on to the general store and refilled his almost empty provision sack, and then rode along to the livery barn, where

Cahill was waiting.

'Describe the horse you swapped for Calder's mount,' Rogan said.

'He picked a roan, and sure knows his horseflesh. I reckoned there was something pushing him because he couldn't wait to hit the saddle and ride out.'

'Show me his tracks. I need to see the prints of the horse he is riding so I can track him. He's led me on a good run and I'd like to nail him before he kills again.'

'Over here.' Cahill crossed to a corral and paused by the gate. Rogan could feel a leaping impatience in his chest but fought down his emotions. Together they studied the many tracks in the dust around the gate until Cahill eventually found some clear prints. 'Here,' he said. 'These are the roan's prints.'

Rogan studied the prints, impressing them on his mind. He spent minutes tracking them away from the corral and, when he was satisfied that he could recognize them anywhere, he went back to his horse, mounted, and rode out, but had only travelled a few yards when Frank Halfnight called his name. He twisted in his saddle to see the town marshal coming along the sidewalk, waving a paper.

'Hold on, Buck,' Halfnight shouted. 'I got a dodger on Jake Yaris that you oughta see before you leave.'

Rogan rode back to Halfnight and stepped down into the dust. Halfnight held out the wanted poster and Rogan scanned it eagerly. There was a small black-and-white drawing of the head and shoulders of a really big man for whom there was a reward of 1000 dollars. Rogan read the description of Yaris with great interest.

'He's a redhead,' he observed.

'That's right, and he wears a red beard. He's got a small crescent scar just above his right eyebrow. You can take that dodger with you, Buck, and look at it until you can pick Yaris out of a crowd, although there ain't many around that look the way he does. If you're going into Indian Territory then keep your lip buttoned about Yaris. He's got an uncanny way of learning about men looking for him, and if he hears about you then you won't have to look too hard for him. You'll wake up one fine morning and find him sitting at the foot of your blankets.'

Rogan smiled grimly. 'If only it could be that easy,' he observed. 'Thanks for the dodger, Frank. If I nail Yaris I'll swing back in this direction and let you know.'

Halfnight grinned and turned away. Rogan remounted and turned his horse to ride out of town. He followed the tracks of the roan Calder was riding.

Once clear of town the tracks showed that Calder was moving fast. Rogan set his face into resolute lines and continued with a stoicism that sprang from hard experience. He was getting closer to Calder all the time, and felt certain he would catch the killer eventually. Just out of Fort Bradnum he hit the border between Arkansas and Indian

Territory, and saw Calder's tracks leading on into the south-west. The killer was apparently turning his back on civilization once more, shunning frequented areas for the lonely trails and comparative safety of the wilderness, and Rogan wondered at the mentality of such men who lived hard and died violently.

The country was wild and desolate. Brush was heavy, impenetrable in places, and silence overhung the area, broken only by the sounds Rogan made in his progress. The afternoon wore on, and he began to make faster time as the brush thinned out. Several times he lost Calder's tracks and had to dismount and search on foot for the elusive prints, but his patience was inexhaustible, his progress inexorable. He was not aware of passing time, being intent only upon his duty, and he spared no effort to gain on his murderous quarry.

He emerged from the brush unexpectedly and reined in quickly to take stock of his surroundings. A movement nearby attracted his gaze. He ducked instinctively and hurled himself from his saddle when a shot crashed out. His pistol was in his hand as he hit the ground and rolled, and he heard the thump of a bullet striking the ground close by.

Levering himself up on his elbows, Rogan peered around. A rider was approaching him fast, having been startled by Rogan's sudden appearance from the brush, and was lifting his pistol for a second shot: no questions asked. Rogan's teeth clicked together as he recognized the bank robber who had escaped from Fort Bradnum.

The foresight of Rogan's big pistol lifted to cover the rider's chest. He squeezed the trigger and the robber was wiped out of his saddle as if struck by a giant hand. He bounced on the hard ground as the shot blasted. His horse turned away abruptly and ran several yards before halting and lowering its head to nibble at the short grass. Sullen echoes faded slowly.

Rogan got to his feet, breathing hard. He looked around quickly, checking for more trouble, but the wilderness was seemingly devoid of life and he turned his gaze to the fallen robber. The man was crumpled on his face, arms outstretched, and his discarded pistol was lying several feet away from his body.

Approaching carefully, gun covering the figure, Rogan turned the man over and looked into a bearded face. The man's eyes were wide, staring sightlessly at the sky. The bullet that had killed him was lodged in the centre of his chest. Rogan looked at the robber's horse, and recognized it as the animal he had seen fast disappearing into Coe's Alley in Fort Bradnum. He nodded in satisfaction, pleased to be able to report a successful conclusion to his brush with the bank robbers.

A faint, unnatural noise alerted Rogan and he swung to look along the line of the brush where it petered out into open countryside. His teeth clicked together when he saw a man standing just inside the brush. The stranger, twenty yards away and almost hidden by the brush, was holding a double-barrelled shotgun, its twin muzzles covering Rogan. A second man, carrying a rifle, was emerging from the same cover.

'Drop the gun,' the second man called.

Rogan opened his fingers without hesitation and his pistol thudded on the ground. The two men came forward, and the way they operated warned Rogan that they knew how to handle this situation. He raised his hands shoulder high and stood motionless, his heart pounding, aware that if he had fallen in with some of the robber's sidekicks then he was in big trouble . . .

2

The man with the pistol approached and picked up Rogan's discarded gun. The second man, holding the shotgun, paused directly in front of Rogan at a distance of ten feet, and the twin muzzles of the fear-some-looking shot-gun gaped at Rogan's chest.

'OK.' The man with the pistols moved around until he could look into Rogan's face. 'So tell us what happened here. We arrived just too late to see the shooting.'

'Who are you?' Rogan countered, not wishing to admit his true identity if these newcomers were badmen.

'I'm Rafe Carter and my pard is Charlie Weedon. We're US deputy marshals out of Fort Smith on the scout for bad men. We spotted the man you just killed way back, and were closing in on him when you crossed our trail and rode into him. So what's your story, mister? We're part of a five-man outfit rounding up all the hardcases we happen to meet.'

Rogan explained tersely, relating his pursuit of Jed Calder and ending with the bank robbery in Fort Bradnum. He revealed his identity and the attitudes of Carter and Weedon mellowed instantly. Carter grinned.

'Show me your credentials,' he said, and Rogan reached into his breast pocket to produce his deputy marshal badge and papers. 'Say, I'm real pleased to meet a man out here who ain't crooked,' Carter mused, returning Rogan's pistol to him. 'So this feller was a bank robber, huh? Take a look at him, Charlie, and see if you can put a name to him.'

The small man with the shotgun came forward and stared intently into the dead man's face before shaking his head.

'No,' he said. 'I've never seen him before. But we can check his face against the wanted posters we got back on the wagon.'

'Good idea.' Carter nodded. 'We'll take him with us. We got eight prisoners with the wagon, Rogan, and we're getting near to the end of our scouting mission. Tomorrow we'll be heading back to Fort Smith. You'll be pushing on after your man, huh?'

Rogan nodded. 'Sure thing! He's pulling away from me all the time.'

'We'll keep an eye open for him,' Carter promised. 'If you get him then drop by Fort Smith and tell the law there. You're getting trouble in Kansas same as we have around here, huh? It looks to me like the badmen have got themselves organized.

'That's what I've heard,' Rogan admitted, 'and if it's true the law will need an army to put a stop to them. Have you heard of Jake Yaris?' He produced the dodger Frank Halfnight had given him and held it out.

Carter studied the drawing of the wanted man. He nodded slowly while reading the description, and grinned when he handed the dodger back to Rogan.

'Yeah, I've heard of Yaris,' he said. 'He's pulled a lot of big jobs around here, but we've never come across him. I've heard tell he's got a big hideout somewhere in Indian Territory. He pays the Indians to watch all approaches to it, and they warn him of any movement towards him by the law. We have made several trips to try and locate him, but he always gives us the slip.'

'It sounds like he's got himself well organized,' Rogan observed. 'But I've been given the chore of finding him, and I'll keep on his trail until I do catch up with him and his gang. Is there anything you can tell me about Yaris? It looks like I'll need all the help I can get to nail him.'

'Rather you than me!' Carter grimaced. 'You should ride to Fort Smith and have a talk with Judge Parker. He's made a big difference against the outlaws since he started operating, and he'd admire to talk to a man like you. Maybe he might come up with an idea that will make your job easier. So long, Rogan! We've got to rattle our hocks. Good hunting.'

'Thanks.' Rogan fetched his horse as the two men prepared to go on, taking the dead bank robber with them.

Alone again, Rogan back-tracked some distance and searched for Calder's prints. The afternoon was wearing away by the time he spotted the faint imprint of an outside edge of a horseshoe in the dust and decided it belonged to Calder's roan. He rode on, his keen eyes picking out tracks leading in the general direction Calder was following.

The brush had given way to short grass, and Rogan made better time. Shadows were closing in when he decided to make camp. He sat his horse for several minutes, scanning his surroundings for signs of a camp, but saw nothing in the desolation of the wilderness and stepped down from his saddle. He prepared to camp for the night but, as he trailed his reins, three shots echoed through the vast space surrounding him.

Three shots were a recognized signal that someone was in trouble. Rogan swung back into his saddle and pointed his horse in the direction from whence the shots had sounded. He rode on, his right hand close to the butt of his pistol, and headed for a stand of trees some 500 yards distant. If someone was in trouble it was probable that Jed Calder was mixed up in it and it was possible the killer was still around.

Rogan spotted the white canvas top of a covered wagon half-hidden by foliage and touched spurs to his horse. A woman holding a rifle appeared from under a tree and stood awaiting his arrival. Rogan pushed his horse faster, and bore down upon the woman to rein in at the last instant. She was old, and covered him with the rifle as he dismounted.

'Are you in trouble, ma'am?' Rogan demanded. 'I heard your shots.'

'My husband has been murdered,' she replied in a wavering tone. 'A man came up with us two hours ago and we stopped to cook him some food. After he had eaten, he pulled a gun and shot my husband in cold blood. He took our money and valuables, and a whole lot of supplies.'

'Can you describe him?'

'He was small, and carried two pistols in crossed cartridge belts. He had a grin on his face the whole time he was here, even when he shot my husband.'

'It sounds like you had a run-in with Jed Calder,' Rogan mused. 'I'm hunting him, and I'm sorry I wasn't closer or I might have prevented your husband's death. Calder is wanted in Kansas for murdering a rancher and his family and several other killings. Where are you heading, ma'am? You're way off the beaten track in these parts.'

'We were making for Guthrie.' She sighed and shook her head.

Rogan led his horse and accompanied the woman through the trees to where a wagon was standing. A two-horse team was unhitched and hobbled nearby. He saw a man stretched out beside the remains of a campfire, and there was a patch of blood on his shirt front.

'He didn't have to shoot Henry,' the woman complained in a high-pitched voice. 'I told him he was welcome to what we had, but he seemed to take great pleasure in killing. I'll never forget the smile on his face when he shot my husband.'

Rogan checked the man, who was dead. He could see that the woman, seemingly in her fifties, was badly shocked. He took the rifle from her and made her sit down by the fire.

'I'm Emily Miller,' she said wearily. 'Henry and I were on our way to settle in Guthrie. It's a fairly new town and has lots of opportunities for hard workers. My son is there already. He's in the lumber business, and wrote us in Idaho saying there were good prospects out here. Now Henry is dead and I don't feel I can go on.'

'I'm Buck Rogan, US Deputy Marshal. I'm sorry, Mrs Miller, that I didn't get here sooner. Can you point out the direction Calder took when he left you?'

'It looked like he was making for Guthrie. There's no other town in that direction. Will you help me hitch the two horses to the wagon? I'll have to go on. My son will worry if I don't show up in Guthrie.'

'Shall I bury Henry under a tree here?' Rogan asked gently. 'You're too far from any town to take him in for a real Christian burial.'

Mrs Miller nodded. She went to the back of the wagon and produced a long-handled sodbuster with a shiny blade. Rogan set to work, dug a grave, and they buried Henry Miller with the minimum of ritual. Then Rogan took some writing paper from his saddlebag and sat down with Mrs Miller to get a statement from her. A long session of questions and answers followed before he was satisfied, and he even managed to get her to list the valuables Henry Miller's killer had stolen, among them a pocket watch Henry had been presented with by an employer before leaving Idaho.

'That watch has Henry's name engraved on the back,' Mrs Miller said shakily, and burst into tears.

Night had fallen as Rogan tried to console Mrs Miller. He unrolled his blankets on the far side of the wagon and turned in, although sleeping was difficult under the circumstances. He lay thinking about the situation for a timeless period, but eventually slept, and the sun was rising when he was awakened by the sound of Mrs Miller preparing breakfast.

After a meal Rogan prepared the wagon for travel and Mrs Miller climbed into the driving seat. She took up a whip and was about to continue her interrupted journey when Rogan caught the sound of a wagon approaching through the trees. He signalled for

Mrs Miller to wait, and turned as a four-horse team hauled a heavily laden wagon into view. Two men were on the driving seat, and one of them reached for a rifle when he saw Rogan.

The wagon halted and Rogan walked close, his right hand down at his side. The two men were hardfaced, suspicious, and the man with the rifle covered Rogan.

'Looks like you've had a spot of trouble,' the driver called. 'That's a new-dug grave over there under that tree.'

Rogan explained what had occurred.

'Where are you heading?' he demanded.

'Guthrie,' the driver replied. 'We're hauling in supplies. This is a regular freight line, and there's a lot of building going on at the end of it.'

'I'm Buck Rogan, Deputy US Marshal. A woman is stranded here who needs to get to Guthrie.' He explained tersely what had occurred. 'I'll be happy if she can travel with you.'

'Sure thing.' The driver swung down

from his high seat. 'I'm Frank Hewitt and this is my pard Joe Garrett. There sure is a whole passel of badmen floating around in this territory, but the law is getting on top of them. There's a US Marshal name of Nix running things in Guthrie, and he's whittling away at the criminals, but until the law takes a good hold folk are being hurt bad by the outlaws.'

They walked across to where Mrs Miller was seated on her wagon, and she agreed to accompany Hewitt and Garrett. Rogan was relieved when they departed with Mrs Miller driving her covered wagon behind the big freighter.

Rogan looked around for Jed Calder's tracks, located them, and resumed his trailing. Nightfall was blanking out his surroundings with shadows when he began to think of making camp, and he selected a spot in a stand of trees where a stream tumbled into a creek. He took care of his horse and knee-hobbled the animal in a patch of lush grass near running water before attending to his own needs.

He ate cold food before turning in, and slept peacefully until the first rays of sunlight lanced through the overhead branches of the trees.

There was no sign of Calder's tracks when he was ready to continue, and Rogan cast around in a wide circle without success. Back-tracking to where he had last seen the prints, he followed them on foot, picking out faint signs that were his only link with the killer. He found a spot where Calder had suddenly turned south, which he had missed in the growing darkness of the previous night, and continued on foot with painstaking care until he was certain Calder had definitely changed direction.

Rogan was accustomed to the exhausting weariness of following a trail; the set-backs which followed when the trail disappeared and the constant searching for fresh prints. He rode through the wilderness in deathly silence, his gaze bent upon the rough ground, his mind trying to out-guess his quarry. He halted at noon for food and continued afterwards through changing country. The short grass gave way to rougher ground — sandy hills, canyons and gullies. He sweated in the heat, buoyed up by the knowledge that he was almost within striking distance of Calder, and if the killer halted for any reason then there would be a grim accounting.

Calder's tracks showed up clear and plain in the thick dust, and Rogan could tell the killer was not far ahead. He was aware that the nearer he got to the man the greater danger there was of being ambushed if Calder was aware of being pursued. The tracks were heading south as if Calder had some definite destination in mind, although Rogan knew there was nothing in that direction but Indian Territory. He could not understand the mentality of the killer, electing to live rough in the wilderness, and wondered if there was a big hideout tucked away somewhere in this barren land where badmen could find sanctuary.

Around the middle of the afternoon the wheel tracks of a large wagon cut across Rogan's trail from east to west. He reined in and gazed at the tracks, wondering at the number of bootprints showing on either side of the wagon. He stood up in his saddle and looked keenly in the direction being taken by the vehicle. The wheel tracks disappeared into a canyon entrance ahead and Rogan, noting that Calder's tracks had turned in the same direction, wondered if the killer was planning to attack yet another wagon.

He entered a defile with high rock walls on each side which widened out into a large canyon and, as he reached the threshold of the canyon, a man armed with a rifle stood up from the cover of a boulder just ahead.

'Don't do anything with your hands,' the man called. 'Just sit still, huh?'

Rogan could see the glint of a law badge on the man's shirtfront and relaxed, keeping his hands well clear of his weapons. A second man appeared from cover on the opposite side of the defile and came forward with a drawn pistol covering Rogan's big figure.

'Get down,' the newcomer ordered, and Rogan dismounted. 'Who are you, mister, and what are you doing here?'

Rogan explained his business and produced his identification. The two lawmen relaxed.

'I'm Bill Howgate,' one said, 'and this is Joe Gill. We're both US deputy marshals. There are about a couple of hundred of us riding this wilderness in small groups to clear it of badmen. We've got ourselves eight prisoners so far, and we're checking out this canyon before we return to Fort Smith because we saw horse tracks heading into it. There are five of us deputies with a wagon, and it looks like we got ourselves a bunch of thieves trapped in here.'

'I met a couple of lawmen two days ago,' Rogan said. 'Rafe Carter and Charlie Weedon! I'm trailing Jed Calder, a killer from Dodge City. He's killed again since leaving Kansas and I want to get him before he murders anyone else. His tracks turned into this canyon ahead of you. It looks like he's interested in those horse tracks you're following.'

'Carter and Weedon are riding with us,' Howgate said. He was tall and broad-shouldered; looked capable of handling any law job. 'They're ahead of us now, taking a look at the rustlers. Frank Shiloh is running things. He's also up ahead. I expect we'll hit the thieves first thing in the morning, unless there's a trail through the canyon and they've kept going. You're welcome to camp with us tonight, Rogan. If your killer is in the canyon then we'll nail him along with the thieves.'

'Thanks. I'll need to check out Calder's tracks,' Rogan said. 'Did any of your deputies manage to identify that bank robber I killed?'

'No. We went through our wanted posters but his face ain't among them. We buried him back along the trail. We'd only take his body along if there was a price on his head. Pete Manning is just ahead with the wagon.' Howgate pointed off to the right. 'I'll walk over there with you. We've got a good haul of prisoners, and the sooner we head back to Fort Smith with them the better. We can't handle more than eight of the buzzards at a time.'

Rogan accompanied the lawman into the canyon, and was surprised when he saw a big wagon with a white canvas top drawn up in a gully. Its four-horse team was knee-hobbled and grazing close by.

'This is our mobile headquarters,' Howgate informed Rogan. 'It's equipped to serve as an office, dormitory, kitchen, arsenal and jail. We don't have a specific mission. We come into Indian Territory on the scout, poking and prying, prowling through canyons like this one for stolen horses and cattle. We investigate suspicious travellers and search shacks for stills and contraband whiskey.'

Rogan saw a man with a law badge on his chest cooking at a fire. He looked closely at the wagon and saw eight prisoners — four on each side, their wrists manacled to a chain fixed to iron rings bolted on the sides of the wagon. The prisoners were seated on the ground, and all looked exhausted.

'What do you think of our private zoo?' Howgate demanded with a laugh. 'They travel like that, chained to the wagon, and have to walk every step of the way. Only the wounded can ride in the wagon. We got all kinds here — the dregs of the West. Eight prisoners are about as many as we can handle at one time so we'll be turning for home pretty soon now. Hey, Pete, we got one extra for supper.'

The cook straightened and came forward to meet Rogan, who explained his mission. He was intrigued by the wagon and the way the deputy marshals were operating. Howgate motioned to him and they walked forward into the canyon and ascended a slight rise that blocked their view of the length of the canyon. They bellied down just before the crest and eased forward to look into the canyon proper, where Rogan saw a herd of some twenty horses about a quarter of a mile ahead, grazing around a stand of cottonwoods. Smoke was rising from a camp that was situated under the trees.

'We won't go any closer,' Howgate said. 'Frank Shiloh will get all the details about those men. They might be honest and on lawful business, although I doubt that. Indian Territory ain't called Hell's Courtyard for nothing. There are about twenty thousand white inhabitants in the Territory, and apart from those shady characters who frequent railroad depots and other legitimate installations there are thousands of others who have circumvented the law prohibiting white men from purchasing Indian land by marrying Indian women, or have signed long leases with Indian landowners and settled down to ranching and farming. Generally the white inhabitants don't like us coming in here to clean up and are hostile; some even help the lawbreakers to evade us.'

Rogan was astounded by the incredible difficulties facing the deputies. They eased back down the slope and returned to the wagon. Looking back, Rogan saw a figure suddenly break cover on the crest of the rise and come hurrying towards them. When the man drew nearer Rogan recognized Weedon, who was carrying his shotgun.

'We'll get some news now,' Howgate said with a grin. 'We'll try to take these thieves without a fight. We never shoot to kill if we can avoid it because every man we take back to stand trial is worth an arrest fee of two dollars, and we don't get anything for corpses unless a dead-or-alive reward has been posted for them by the railroads or stage companies or some civil authority.'

Weedon, carrying his shotgun across his chest, came at a half-run towards the camp, and grinned when he recognized Rogan.

'Rafe and Frank are still watching

that bunch,' he reported when he arrived. 'They're horse-thieves all right. Two-Fingered Jack Kroll is with them, and he'd steal his own mother's horse, if she had one. We've been after Kroll and his bunch for a long time, and it looks like their luck has finally run out. There are four of them, and there's a newcomer with them.' Weedon looked at Rogan and grinned. 'He's a small man, wearing twin pistols, who grins all the time. Frank reckons it's the guy you told us about, Rogan.'

'Jed Calder,' Rogan said eagerly. 'I followed his trail in this direction. So I've caught up with him at last.'

'Frank reckons we'll go for them after dark, when the moon comes up,' Weedon said. 'They're set in their camp until morning. As far as we can tell there's only one way out of this canyon and we're sitting across it. Frank will be back shortly. He reckons when we've taken care of this bunch we'll head back to Fort Smith with our prisoners.'

Rogan stood for a moment, thinking

about the trail he had followed from Dodge City, and was thankful it had at last reached its conclusion, but he would not be satisfied until he had put handcuffs on Jed Calder. He went to take care of his horse and then sat down on his blankets beside the campfire. He needed to confront Calder and capture him, and would have to contain his impatience and work with this tough law party, which seemed to know exactly what it was doing.

Frank Shiloh and Rafe Carter turned up suddenly, easing over the rise ahead and coming swiftly towards the camp. Carter greeted Rogan with a grin, his face showing pleasure when he introduced Rogan to the chief deputy, and Shiloh shook hands with Rogan. There was an air of grim efficiency about Shiloh, who was a medium-sized man with piercing blue eyes and a determined manner.

'We'll gather them in when they've settled down for the night,' Shiloh said.

'You'll go along with us, Rogan? It looks like your man is there with the thieves.'

'Sure thing!' Rogan replied eagerly. 'I've got another job to handle after taking Calder. Can you tell me anything about an outlaw hideout in the Territory, run by a hardcase named Jake Yaris? I've heard that a great number of badmen rest up there when they're not robbing and killing in Kansas and Arkansas.'

'I've heard tell of such a place but there's no proof it exists,' Shiloh said. 'We keep our eyes open for that sort of thing, but so far we've usually picked up our quota of badmen before we get too far into the Territory. One of these days I suspect we will have enough men to be able to make a clean sweep right through the country, and that should put an end to this bad situation.'

They settled down to a meal and then waited out the remaining time, nerves tightening and determination filling them. Rogan checked his pistol before stretching out on his blanket to take a well-deserved rest until Shiloh called his group together. Pete Manning remained behind in the camp to watch their prisoners, and Rogan followed the four resolute lawmen into the growing shadows. The time for action had arrived.

3

A faint crescent of the moon showed remotely above the canyon wall as the lawmen made their way to the camp of the horse-thieves. Stars became more distinct as shadows crowded the rough ground. A cool breeze blew into Rogan's face from the camp and he caught a tang of wood smoke and cooked food in its intangible breath. Shiloh and his three sidekicks proved they were well experienced as they closed in on the camp. They walked in single file with Rogan bringing up the rear, and Shiloh, leading, made his way to the left of the stand of trees to keep the camp between the stolen horses and themselves.

The reddish gleam of a low fire showed between the trees, and Rogan heard the sound of running water somewhere close by. Shiloh left the deputies crouching in the shadows while he moved forward alone into the fringe of the trees. Complete silence pervaded the canyon. Rogan had drawn his pistol, and was waiting stolidly for the action to commence. Shiloh was gone for what seemed an interminable time, and returned suddenly, materializing out of the heavy shadows under the tress. He was carrying an inert figure across one shoulder, and dumped it on the ground at Rogan's feet.

'It's OK,' he said in an undertone. 'They're all asleep in their blankets. I took care of this guard, and his hands are cuffed behind his back. We better move in and get the drop on them before he comes to and starts yelling. Two of you work around to their rear and cut them off. When you're in position I'll call them out, and we'll try to do this without shooting.'

Two of the deputies moved away silently into the darkness. Rogan took a fresh grip on his pistol and steeled himself for action. He wanted to take

Jed Calder prisoner, and nothing else mattered but that the killer was apprehended, either dead or alive. Moments later, Shiloh led them into the sleeping camp, and the night seemed to take on a degree of insidious tension.

Their eyes were accustomed to the shadows as they closed in. An owl hooted mournfully from a high branch of a cottonwood and a saddle horse stamped in the undergrowth. Presently, Rogan saw the campfire in a clearing and spotted blankets unrolled around it. They closed in, and the two deputies who had gone around the camp appeared from the further side, firelight glinting on their ready weapons. The humped figures in the blankets did not move, but Rogan was aware that men like these were used to sleeping with a pistol in their hands, and their reaction to any disturbance would be instant hostility.

The deputies each covered a sleeping figure. Rogan bent over the nearest as

Shiloh called in an echoing voice.

'This is the law. You're surrounded. Sit up, and nobody reaches for a gun.'

The reaction to the command was instantaneous. All four figures came awake and began to spring up from their blankets. Pistols glinted in the low fire-light. Rogan saw with grim satisfaction that the man he was covering was Jed Calder, and the killer's instinctive response was to lift a pistol he had been clutching in his hand while asleep.

Rogan kicked away Calder's gun hand before the weapon could line up on him and struck shrewdly with his six-gun. His barrel slammed against Calder's skull and the killer subsided without a sound. Rogan wrenched the gun out of Calder's inert hand and looked around to see that the other thieves in the camp had all been disarmed without resistance. They were, without exception, sitting up in their blankets with their hands raised in token of surrender, their expressions showing shock at the swift turn of events.

'Howdy, Two-Finger.' Shiloh's tone was filled with grim satisfaction. 'Looks like your luck finally ran out, huh? You sure gave us a good run over the past two years. Cuff'em, men, and we'll take them back to the wagon. In the morning we'll be heading for Fort Smith.'

Rogan was already putting handcuffs on Jed Calder. The killer was coming to his senses, and by the time he was aware of what was happening he was securely manacled. Rogan pulled him to his feet.

'Jed Calder, I'm arresting you for murder,' Rogan said sharply. 'I'll be taking you back to Dodge City to stand trial.'

'You got the wrong man,' Calder replied. 'I've never been in Kansas.'

'You murdered Henry Miller a few days ago,' Rogan responded. 'I got you dead to rights, mister.'

'I ain't murdered anyone,' Calder snarled.

Shiloh threw an armful of twigs on

the low fire which blazed up to throw uncertain light through the camp.

'Search 'em,' Shiloh ordered, and the deputies complied eagerly.

Rogan searched Calder for hidden weapons, found a short-barrelled pistol in the killer's back pocket, and took a pocket watch from a breast pocket. Turning to the leaping flames of the fire, Rogan read the inscription on the back of the watch.

'This watch has Henry Miller's name on it,' Rogan said. 'Mrs Miller said her husband's watch was among the items you stole from her.'

Shiloh came to Rogan's side, his teeth glinting in the firelight as he grinned.

'Is this your man, Rogan?' he demanded.

'Yep! Jed Calder. I've taken this pocket watch off him. It's got the name of Henry Miller on the back. Calder stole it when he murdered Miller. I have a statement made by Mrs Miller in which she lists several items taken by

Calder. I guess this watch is all the proof I need.'

'Where is Mrs Miller now?' Shiloh asked.

'On her way to Guthrie with a couple of freighters.'

'You'll need to fetch her to Fort Smith to give evidence against Calder even though you have her statement.' Shiloh shook his head. 'Judge Parker will want to talk to any witnesses to the murders Calder has committed.'

'I'm planning to head back to Kansas in the morning,' Rogan said instantly. 'Calder is wanted for murdering a whole family near Dodge City.'

'You said he murdered Henry Miller a few days ago so he'll have to stand trial for that in Fort Smith. That's the way the law stands in Arkansas. You won't be heading back to Kansas until Judge Parker has pronounced the death sentence on Calder and it has been carried out; and the judge will certainly want evidence from Mrs Miller in person

55

despite that statement she made to you.'

'You got the wrong man,' Calder snarled. 'I never killed anyone.'

Rogan knew enough about the law to accept Shiloh's words.

'Will you take Calder on to Fort Smith?' he asked. 'I'd better ride after Mrs Miller before she gets too far ahead on the trail.'

'Now you're talking.' Shiloh grinned. 'We'll take good care of Calder. He'll be in jail in Fort Smith when you get there. Give me Mrs Miller's statement before you leave in the morning. I'll need it to hold Calder for Miller's murder. Judge Parker is a stickler for the letter of the law. We always have to get everything just right.'

The prisoners were taken back to the wagon, chained to the vehicle, and the camp settled down for the night. The deputies took it in turns to guard the prisoners, and Rogan stood watch in the small hours. Frank Shiloh ran his camp with the precision of a military operation, and as the sun came up the wagon was ready to move off in the direction of Fort Smith, all prisoners accounted for.

Rogan gave Mrs Miller's statement to Frank Shiloh, and the stolen items listed in it were matched with what had been found in Calder's possession. Rogan shook hands with Shiloh and watched the cavalcade of the law move off to the east. He took particular satisfaction from watching Jed Calder stumbling along in chains beside the lurching wagon, and the vicious killer turned his head for a malevolent look at Rogan just before the vehicle disappeared over a nearby rise.

It was difficult for Rogan to accustom himself to riding without checking the ground for tracks, and he made good time as he rode back to where Henry Miller was lying in his lonely grave. He stopped briefly beside the grave to rest his horse and eat, and when he rode on again he estimated that he was some twenty miles behind Mrs Miller's wagon.

Travelling at a mile-eating lope, Rogan did not halt to make camp until the shadows of approaching night prevented him from following wheel tracks. He had made good time during the daylight hours, and expected to catch up with the freighters around noon the next day. He slept fitfully, and was ready to hit the trail again when the sun came up. He followed the wheel tracks at a fast clip, eager to get to Mrs Miller.

At noon a wisp of smoke stained the sky ahead of Rogan, just behind a rise, and he frowned as he sent his horse up an incline to rein in on the crest. His narrowed gaze picked out the blackened ruins of a burnt-out wagon at the bottom of the slope and he dropped his hand to the butt of his pistol as he descended. There was no sign of Mrs Miller, the big freight wagon or the two freighters, Hewitt and Garrett. Only the acrid smell of burning was apparent.

Rogan descended the slope warily his

eyes and ears strained for the slightest hostile movement or sound. He reined in beside the wagon, which had been reduced almost to a heap of smoking ashes. Before he dismounted, Rogan's keen gaze searched for signs of Mrs Miller, either dead or alive, but saw nothing of her. He spotted several empty cartridge cases lying on the ground as he stepped down from his horse, trailed his reins and stooped to check the dusty ground for prints. The first thing he saw was a mass of horse tracks where at least eight riders had swooped from cover on the left to converge on the two wagons. The big freight wagon had turned south, its wheel tracks rutted in the ground.

Rogan walked around the scene, trying to read what had happened from a confusion of boot tracks. Obviously Hewitt and Garrett had been taken by surprise, and Rogan was shocked when he spotted that the riders who had ambushed the wagons were riding unshod horses. He wondered if he had come upon the murderous work of Indians!

He climbed back into his saddle and set off to trail the freight wagon, aware that it could not be far ahead. He rode fast, his right hand close to the butt of his pistol, and barely thirty minutes had elapsed when he peered over a crest and saw the wagon lumbering along with two men on the driving seat and two riders escorting it. Rogan was relieved to see that the strangers were not Indians, but he saw no signs of Hewitt, Garrett, or Mrs Miller.

Sending his horse off to the right, Rogan circled the wagon and approached it from the south, crossing a ridge to bear down on it head on, pistol in his hand. He was spotted before he could get within fifty yards of the vehicle, and came under immediate fire from three of the strangers. He flattened himself in his saddle and rode fast to close in on the wagon, ignoring the ominous crackle of closely passing lead and levelling his big pistol to engage the hostile strangers. This was action the way he preferred it.

The two riders escorting the wagon came towards him, shooting wildly. Rogan snapped off a shot that struck the right-hand rider and dumped him out of his saddle. The man bounced on the hard ground and did not move again. Rogan felt a bullet plunk through the crown of his hat and swung his pistol, triggering the weapon as the foresight lined up on the second rider. The weapon blasted and the man fell sideways out of his saddle. Rogan swung his horse to the right, holding his reins in his left hand, and his big six-shooter lifted to cover the two men on the driving seat of the wagon. One of them was working the lever of a rifle and Rogan triggered a shot into his chest.

The driver had his hands filled with four sets of reins, and hauled the team to a halt as his companion fell forward across the backs of the two rear horses before dropping to the ground. He raised his hands without being told, and sat motionless, his eyes filled with wariness. Rogan rode in close, covering the man.

'Who are you and what are you doing driving this wagon?' Rogan demanded. His voice was husky from the gun smoke he had inhaled.

'Who in hell are you?' the man countered. He was tall and thin with a lean face and unshaven cheeks; dressed in dusty range clothes.

'Buck Rogan, US Deputy Marshal. Why are you driving this wagon?'

'I'm Jake Peck, and it's my job to drive this wagon,' the man said tensely. 'We've been to Guthrie to get supplies for the Spooner ranch, which is a couple of miles south of here.'

'You're lying!' Rogan snapped. 'Two days ago this rig was being driven by two men, Hewitt and Garrett, and the burnt-out wagon on your back trail belonged to a woman, Mrs Miller. So where are those three people? I didn't see any sign of them at the scene of the hold-up. Eight of you held up this rig, so what happened to the other four men? My guess is that they went on to the ranch you mentioned, taking three prisoners with them.'

The man's expression informed Rogan that he had hit upon the truth. He could see that the wagon was following a regular trail south and motioned with his pistol.

'Get down and be quick about it,' Rogan rapped, and the man sprang down from the high seat. 'Get rid of your gun before you make a fatal mistake and try to use it.'

Peck disarmed himself and stood watching Rogan intently, his narrowed eyes filled with desperation. Rogan dismounted and reached into a saddle-bag for a pair of handcuffs. He snapped a cuff around Peck's right wrist and then, under the menace of his levelled pistol, led the man to the back of the wagon and snapped the other cuff around a metal strut.

'You're gonna have to wait here until

I can get back to you,' Rogan said. He swung into his saddle and rode off with Peck's protests ringing in his ears.

In a matter of minutes Rogan could see the roofs of several buildings in the distance. He circled the ranch at a walk, and had reached a position off the rear right-hand corner of an adobe house when he saw Hewitt, Garrett and Mrs Miller appear around the opposite rear corner of the building. The two freighters had their hands raised and, as they cleared the corner, three riders appeared behind them, all holding levelled pistols.

Rogan was filled with horror as he read the scene. The three riders were urging their prisoners along in the direction of a gully some yards out from the house, and their intention was obvious. Hewitt turned his head and said something to the men. One of the riders jumped his horse forward and knocked the freighter to the ground. Hewitt struggled up and continued walking.

Sliding his Winchester from its scabbard under his right leg, Rogan jacked a shell into the breech and lifted the long gun to his right shoulder. Mrs Miller fell to her knees and Hewitt and Garrett reached down to help her up. When one of the riders levelled his pistol at Mrs Miller, Rogan started shooting.

The flat crack of the Winchester echoed across the range. Rogan saw his target pitch sideways out of the saddle, and switched his aim to the second man. He fired so rapidly the noise of the shots rolled together in one long thunderous sound. All three riders vacated their saddles in swift succession. Hewitt and Garrett swung about, their hands still raised, shocked into momentary immobility. Then Hewitt dived for a fallen pistol and snatched it up before grabbing at the reins of the restless horses. Garrett joined him.

Rogan rode forward. Garrett helped Mrs Miller into a saddle and they rode towards Rogan at a canter.

'Let's get out of here,' Rogan said harshly as they reached him. 'Your wagon is about a mile back along the trail.'

'I'm glad to see you again, Marshal,' Hewitt gasped. 'They were going to shoot us in cold blood! They stole our wagon!'

'How many men are on the ranch?' Rogan asked.

'I saw about six more,' Garrett replied.

They rode fast away from the ranch, and Rogan dropped back slightly to watch their back trail. He assumed that the men on the ranch thought his shooting was the sound of the prisoners being killed, and began to breathe more easily when they had put distance between themselves and the ranch.

The wagon was where Rogan had left it, and Jake Peck was standing forlornly at the rear, cuffed to the vehicle.

'Get the wagon turned and make tracks out of here,' Rogan said briskly. 'Mrs Miller, I want you to ride with me. I caught the killer who murdered your husband, but I shall need you to stand up in court in Fort Smith and tell the judge what happened. Will you do that? I'll see that you get to Guthrie safely after the trial; after Jed Calder has been hanged for murdering your husband.'

Mrs Miller nodded. She seemed badly shocked. Her eyes were narrowed, over-bright, and she was trembling.

'We got more trouble,' Hewitt called, and pointed to their back trail.

Rogan looked around and saw five riders appearing on a crest.

'That big guy in the centre with the black patch over his left eye is Spooner. He owns that ranch back there,' Hewitt said. 'He told those three men you killed to shoot us and bury our bodies in a gully. We'd be dead now if you hadn't showed up, Marshal.'

'Get the wagon moving,' Rogan ordered. 'Arm yourselves and be ready to fight. I'll take on these killers if they want to push their luck. Mrs Miller, go with the wagon. I'll catch up with you later and then we'll ride to Fort Smith.'

The wagon was turned and moved out fast. Rogan followed until they passed over a crest and were out of sight of the hardcases. He dismounted in cover, grasped his rifle, bellied up to the crest to observe, and nodded when he saw the riders coming towards him at a fast clip.

The big man wearing the black patch was urging his companions into a gallop. Rogan waited for the group to draw within range before lifting his rifle. He glanced along the sights and lined them up on Spooner. The Winchester recoiled when he squeezed the trigger, and Spooner reared back in his saddle as if he had been struck by lightning. The crack of the shot echoed away into the vast distance. Rogan watched intently and saw Spooner lose his balance and slide backwards out of his saddle. His feet caught up in his stirrups and he hung head downwards while his horse galloped on.

The four survivors reacted instantly. They pulled their horses to a halt and then turned to gallop back out of range. Spooner's horse kept running, swerving to bypass Rogan's position. Rogan resumed shooting. He hit three more riders and they vacated their saddles to litter the dusty ground. The fifth rider managed to pass over an opposite rise before Rogan could line up his sights for a parting shot. Dull echoes drifted away across the illimitable wilderness.

Rogan felt no compunction for the dead men. They had been intent upon murdering innocent folk, and Rogan was in the grim business of protecting and defending people going about their lawful business. He eased back from his position and back to his horse. His ears were ringing from the shooting as he rode fast to overtake the wagon.

He watched his back trail for signs of pursuit, but there was no movement behind, and he pushed on until he sighted the wagon. Hewitt was driving his team at a fast pace, but slowed the

69

horses when he saw Rogan approaching. Mrs Miller was riding a horse behind the wagon, just behind the lumbering figure of Jake Peck, who was being pulled along, his right hand attached by the handcuff to the vehicle. Two spare horses were also tethered to the wagon. Mrs Miller turned a tense face towards Rogan as he reached her.

'I don't think you'll have any more trouble from that bunch,' Rogan told Hewitt as he rode alongside the wagon. 'I'll cut off now with Mrs Miller, and I'll take my prisoner with me. You'd better keep your eyes peeled for any more trouble. There's no telling what lies ahead of you. This sure is bad country. There seems to be a badman behind every bush.'

Hewitt nodded, his face grimly set. 'We've never had so much trouble on a trip before,' he said, hauling on his reins and pulling his team to a halt. 'I'll hire a couple of outriders after this.'

'Good luck.' Rogan reined about and rode in beside Mrs Miller. 'Are you ready to ride with me, ma'am?' he asked.

Mrs Miller nodded. She seemed incapable of speech at that moment. Rogan dismounted, freed Peck from the wagon, cuffed his hands behind his back, and pushed him into the saddle of a spare horse. He glanced around to get his bearings and then turned east to ride at a canter.

They camped that night in a draw, but Rogan did not get much sleep. He lay in his blankets, catnapping for an hour at a time, and was up and preparing breakfast before the sun showed over the eastern horizon. Mrs Miller seemed to have recovered somewhat from her deep shock, although she remained mainly silent. The prisoner was sullen and had a perpetual scowl on his face. They broke camp and continued, and Rogan was careful to avoid the spot on the trail where Henry Miller was buried.

It was late afternoon when Rogan spotted the law wagon ahead. He stood up in his stirrups to gaze at the lumbering vehicle and the prisoners walking alongside it, chained securely to the sides. Two deputy marshals were riding in close attendance, and the wagon halted when Rogan's approach was spotted, the prisoners instantly dropping to the ground to rest their weary limbs.

Rogan rode in close, looking for Jed Calder's small figure, but there was no sign of the killer or Frank Shiloh, the chief deputy. Howgate swung his horse and waited for Rogan and Mrs Miller to reach him. His face wore a harsh expression as he lifted a hand in greeting.

'We've had some bad trouble, Rogan,' Howgate said. 'I don't know how it happened, but during last night your prisoner Calder and three of our prisoners got out of their chains. They stumbled over Shiloh in his blanket and killed him with a rock before taking horses and riding off. Weedon and Carter took up their trail this morning and we haven't seen hide or hair of them since. I'm mighty sorry your man was among those who gave us the slip. We never heard a thing, and didn't know until sun-up that four of the prisoners had got away; then we found Shiloh dead in his blankets.'

Rogan gazed at the deputy in disbelief, shocked by the grim news. He was angered by the knowledge that Calder had once again eluded him.

4

'How did the prisoners get out of their handcuffs?' Rogan asked, his mind seething with conjecture as he struggled with his shock.

Howgate shook his head. 'We got no idea. We've never had any trouble like this before. The cuff that was around Calder's wrist was unlocked when we looked at it, but it doesn't seem likely he had a key on him, huh? But we reckon someone did, and he set the others free. Personally I reckon Two-Finger Jack Kroll was behind it. Him and two of the others who escaped were working together as a gang when we caught them, and Kroll is a real slippery customer. Those three and Calder were on the same side of the wagon, so I reckon that's why they turned Calder loose when they pulled out.'

'Weedon and Carter are following

their tracks, huh?' Rogan demanded.

Howgate nodded, clearly puzzled by the successful escape of the prisoners. 'Weedon and Carter are good men.' He shook his head again. 'I think they'll recapture those four.'

'I wouldn't bet on it if Calder is still with them,' Rogan asserted. 'Will you take Mrs Miller to Fort Smith with you? I'll get on Calder's trail. I shouldn't want anyone else to take him.'

'Sure thing! If you follow our wheel tracks you'll come to the spot where we buried Shiloh at dawn this morning. It must be ten, mebbe twelve miles back. I'm about to make camp for the night. Mrs Miller will be welcome to travel with us.'

'Thanks. I'll see you in Fort Smith when I've got Calder again.' Rogan turned his horse and rode in beside Mrs Miller to acquaint her with the situation. She merely nodded when Rogan said he had to leave, and he swung his horse and began to back-track the wheel ruts of the law wagon.

Rogan rode fast through the late afternoon, his determination thrusting aside burgeoning disappointment at Calder's escape. The thick shadows of approaching night were closing in to blot out the wild scenery by the time he reached the lonely spot where Frank Shiloh was buried. The sun disappeared and darkness fell. Rogan made camp and sat by a small fire while he ate cold food and drank strong coffee, his thoughts rambling over the situation. In the morning he would take up Calder's trail again, and stick with it through hell itself to get his man. He turned into his blankets and slept deeply until the rising sun struck his face and awakened him.

With the sun climbing above the eastern horizon, Rogan could see a mass of tracks in the dust and stood looking intently at them, his practised eyes reading the story of what had happened during the previous night. He saw where four horses had been led from the camp, followed by two horses travelling alone, and tracked the prints until they were well clear of the campsite. He noted where the escaping prisoners had mounted, and deeper tracks showed where Calder and his new associates had galloped away.

Rogan went back for his horse, mounted and set out to follow. Carter and Weedon had ridden to one side of the tracks, which pleased Rogan for he could plainly see the four sets of tracks of the badmen. The tracks suddenly diverged from the wheel tracks of the wagon and cut away south-west. Rogan pushed his horse along at a fast clip, determined to recapture Calder.

Six hours later he reined up on a ridge and found himself looking down at a jumble of adobe buildings which formed a cattle ranch. A dozen horses were in a corral, but there was no movement around the dusty yard. The tracks Rogan had followed were heading straight into the yard, and the two sets of following hoofprints showed that

Carter and Weedon had circled the spread.

Looking around intently, Rogan gradually became aware that he was at the Spooner ranch, where Hewitt, Garrett and Mrs Miller had been taken after the freight wagon was hijacked. He moved in the direction where he had fought off Spooner and his killers and came to the spot where Spooner and three of his men lay dead. He returned to his vantage point overlooking the ranch. It was obvious that Two-Finger Jack Kroll was familiar with this area.

The afternoon was almost past and the sun was low over in the west when Rogan dismounted out of sight of the ranch to await the onset of night. He used his hat to give his horse some water from his canteen and then off-saddled and knee-hobbled the animal and let it graze on the sparse vegetation. He ate cold food and drank sparingly from his canteen, not daring to light a fire to make coffee in case his smoke was spotted.

As full darkness came he was sitting on a rock cleaning his pistol and, when the shadows were thick enough for his purpose, Rogan walked to the ranch, aware that one window of the adobe building was illuminated by feeble yellow lamplight. He recalled that one killer at least had escaped unharmed from the small killing ground where Spooner had died.

Rogan's boots made no sound in the thick dust of the yard. He approached the house from the side and gained the nearest front corner without incident, pausing often and listening intently for suspicious sound. He fully expected to find a watchful guard lurking in the shadows, but saw and heard nothing, and stood at the corner, gun in hand and ready for action.

The lighted window drew him and he edged closer to it, moving an inch at a time. When he was standing beside the window he craned forward to take a quick look inside the lighted room, and a grin stretched his lips when he saw

Jed Calder seated at a table with three other men, one of whom had just two fingers on his left hand. They were eating a hot meal which had evidently been served by a stranger who was standing in the background watching the quartet eating.

Rogan drew back, wondering where Carter and Weedon were. He had seen their tracks close to the ranch and guessed they were near by; no doubt waiting for what they judged would be the right moment to attempt the recapture of these hardmen. He turned slightly, placed his back to the adobe wall and looked around into the shadows. If he could join up with Carter and Weedon they would have a good chance of succeeding in their quest.

The heavy silence overhanging the ranch was suddenly broken by shouts that were followed instantly by a clatter of many hoofs on hard ground. Rogan glanced in the direction of the nearby corral although he could see nothing.

He heard the horses in the corral gallop away from the ranch, the drumming of their hoofs punctuated by shrill yells. The voices cut off suddenly, and then the hoofbeats faded away and full silence returned, seemingly heavier than before.

Rogan eased back around the corner of the house until he was concealed. There was no reaction from the men in the house although they must have heard the commotion caused by the running horses. He waited, listening intently, certain that Calder would have left the house by the back door. He assumed that Carter and Weedon had chased off the horses, and wondered what the two deputy marshals would do next.

A stealthy boot scraped hard ground just in front of the house and Rogan flattened himself against the corner, not wishing to attract fire from the two lawmen. A pistol blasted suddenly, hurling echoes through the night, and muzzle flame spurted from the window

Rogan had used to look into the ranch house. Then a spate of shots hammered raucously and the yard was covered by criss-crossing slugs in a lethal hail of probing death.

Rogan pulled out immediately, aware that any movement he made could draw fire from either side. He retreated to halfway along the side of the house before moving out to the edge of the yard. Shooting continued rapidly as he faded into the shadows and moved around to the front of the house.

Two pistols were shooting at the house from vantage points in the yard, and Rogan pin-pointed the positions of the two lawmen. He waited for a lull in the shooting, hunkered down in cover, and, as the gun echoes faded, called in a low, insistent tone.

'Carter, Weedon, this is Buck Rogan. The four escapees are inside the house.'

'Rogan,' Carter replied instantly. 'I reckoned you would show up. If you'll cover the back of the house and cut 'em off we'll wear them down. We'll rush them shortly. I'd like to take 'em alive if we can.'

Two guns opened fire again from the windows in the front of the house. Rogan moved away and hurried to the rear, which was dark and silent. He found cover and dropped into it, lying with his pistol cocked. Shooting continued at the front of the building.

The creak of a door opening alerted Rogan and he got up on one knee to observe. Dense shadows blanketed the rear of the house and he narrowed his eyes in an attempt to pierce the gloom. He spotted a faint movement and raised his pistol when the pale oval of a face peered out of the back door. Rogan waited tensely, covering the spot. For long moments nothing happened, and then a figure slipped out of the doorway and, bent almost double, began to run for the nearest cover.

'Hold it!' Rogan yelled. 'I got you covered.'

The escaping man fired instantly, using Rogan's voice as a guide, and a slug crackled by Rogan's head. He fired instantly and the figure sprawled headlong and lay still. Rogan waited, gun poised. The shooting at the front of the house petered out and a tense silence ensued.

Rogan closed in, watching the back door, his eyes fairly well accustomed to the shadows. He eased to his right to approach the fallen figure, caught a glint of starlight on a discarded pistol, and kicked the weapon away before dropping to one knee beside the sprawled man. He used his left hand to check out the motionless figure and his fingers found a patch of blood on the side of the man's neck. He pressed his hand against the chest and found no heartbeat.

He could not tell if the man was Jed Calder, but the dead man's identity was unimportant at that moment. He arose, approached the back door and, as he reached it, heard Rafe Carter calling his name from inside the house.

'Rogan, we got three of them. Calder

is not here. Come on in.'

Rogan released his pent-up breath in a long sigh as he entered the house, calling to Carter to announce his presence. An inner door opened at the front of the house and lamplight shone along the passage in which Rogan stood. Carter appeared in the doorway, gun in hand.

'We had to kill two of them, but we got Two-Finger Kroll dead to rights,' Carter said. 'He's got a slug in his right arm for his trouble. How'd you make out?'

'I nailed someone who ran out the back door,' Rogan replied. 'I'll need a light to see who it is.'

'Be right with you.' Carter came along the passage with a lamp in his hand. 'We got here before sundown and saw our prisoners making themselves at home. Two-Finger Jack looked like he knew his way around. This is the Spooner ranch, where you had your run-in with Spooner's bunch. We have known for some time that Spooner needed watching, and it looks like he finally reached the end of his rope, huh?'

'He was a cold-blooded killer,' Rogan observed.

Rogan covered the deputy marshal as they went out back, and they paused beside the motionless figure of the man Rogan had shot.

'It ain't Calder,' Rogan observed, his tone laced with a thread of relief. 'This man was serving our escaped prisoners with a meal when I arrived. I saw him through the front window. He must be one of Spooner's crew. One of them got away from me when I shot it out with Spooner.'

'So where is Calder?' Carter looked around into the impenetrable shadows.

'There's nothing we can do about him until sun-up,' Rogan mused, 'but he won't get far without a horse. I'll pick up his trail in the morning.'

They returned to the house and Rogan saw Charlie Weedon sitting on a chair in the big front room overlooking the porch, wrapping a bandage around his left bicep. Weedon's shotgun was lying close to hand on the table in front of the deputy. Weedon grinned at Rogan.

'We were expecting you to show up on Calder's trail,' Weedon said. 'Did you get him?'

'No. He must have got out through a side window,' Rogan observed. 'I'll pick up his tracks in the morning.'

He saw two bodies lying on the floor near the front windows, and Two-Finger Kroll was sitting on the floor in a corner, his wrists cuffed, his right sleeve stained with blood. Rogan crossed to the badman and looked down at him. Kroll was sullen-faced; his dark eyes narrowed.

'Which of you had the handcuff key that was used for the escape from the law wagon?' Rogan asked, 'and who killed Frank Shiloh?'

'You don't expect me to tell you anything, do you?' Kroll countered, his face twisted into a sneer of defiance.

Rafe Carter came across to Rogan's

side and kicked Kroll's outstretched left leg.

'Keep a civil tongue, Kroll,' he rasped, 'and answer the man's questions. You've got a lot to talk about, and you better unbutton your lip or I'll break one of your legs and make you walk all the way to Fort Smith.'

'You'll hang me when we get there,' Kroll snarled, 'so I got nothing to say except it's a long way to the jail.'

'You won't get another chance to escape,' Carter said heavily. He kicked Kroll's leg again. 'Who killed Frank Shiloh?'

'It wasn't me,' Kroll replied. 'I wouldn't have killed him while he was sleeping. I would have wakened him so he could see who was sending him to hell.'

'So Calder did the killing, huh?' Rogan asked.

'That's how it happened,' Kroll admitted.

'And how did you get out of your handcuffs?' Carter persisted.

Kroll grinned. 'It ain't for me to say. I reckon it's up to you to find out. Ask yourself if one of your deputies turned us loose for a pay-off?'

'That's a damn lie!' Carter grasped Kroll by the shoulders and lifted him bodily from the floor. He slammed Kroll against a wall and hit him with his right fist as he slumped forward. Kroll fell senseless to the floor and Carter bent over him, searching him efficiently, and when he straightened he was holding up a handcuffs key.

'How did he get hold of that?' Rogan demanded.

'I'd like to think someone dropped it and Kroll picked it up.' Carter spoke through his teeth. 'I will find out though, and there'll be hell to pay if one of the men got careless. It cost Frank Shiloh his life, and I never knew a better lawman than Frank.'

'You'll take Kroll back to the wagon in the morning, huh?' Rogan queried.

'Sure.' Carter heaved a sigh. 'I guess you can handle Calder on your own. I sure hope you won't have too much trouble catching him again.'

'I'll get him.' Rogan turned to the door. 'I'd better fetch my horse and get ready for an early start in the morning. It's likely Calder will find one of those horses you ran off. I'm gonna have to track down every last one of them to check.'

'I'll have some grub ready when you get back,' Carter told him.

Rogan left the house by the back door and stood for several moments in the shadows, looking around intently, his ears strained for unnatural sounds. He knew enough about Jed Calder to take all the precautions he could think of. Calder wouldn't move far on foot, and the killer had enough nerve to stick around and try to pick off the lawmen in the morning.

He moved slowly through the shadows, gun in hand, listening intently for unnatural noise from his surroundings. The darkness was relieved somewhat by starshine, which gave enough light for him to make out nearer features. He slowed to one step at a time as he neared the spot where he had left his horse, his nerves taut, hair-triggered for instant action. He heard nothing suspicious, and was shocked when he eventually reached the spot where his horse had been hobbled to find the animal gone.

Aware that the horse would not stray, Rogan concluded that Calder must have chanced upon the animal. He returned to the ranch with the cold fingers of disappointment clutching at his chest. Calder was free and well-mounted. The killer had the whole of the Territory in which to conceal himself, and Rogan gritted his teeth in frustration at the thought of having to start his manhunt all over again.

'I'm real sorry for the trouble you're getting,' Carter said as he ladled food on to a plate for Rogan. 'You would have been better off if you hadn't met us.'

Rogan smiled and ate his meal,

afterwards checking through the house. Neither Carter nor Weedon would agree to him taking a turn at guarding Two-Finger Kroll.

'He's our prisoner and we're responsible for him,' Carter said. 'You better get yourself a good night's sleep, Rogan. There's no telling when you'll be able to rest easy when you hit Calder's trail tomorrow.'

Rogan turned in on a bunk in a bedroom and slept until morning. He arose at first light and went outside to check for prints before Carter had prepared breakfast. He walked around the outside of the ranch house, and found footprints below a ground-floor window in the side of the building where someone had left the house in a hurry. He followed the prints to the nearest cover, a shack by the corral where saddles and riding tackle were stored, and drew his gun before entering.

The shack was empty except for riding equipment. Rogan followed the prints around to the rear and saw where

Calder had paused by the corral. It pleased him to think of his quarry being afoot, but the loss of his own horse added to the odds against catching Calder again. If the killer had taken the bay then Rogan had to get himself another mount as soon as possible.

He followed the prints around the corral, aware that Calder had played smart, moving in a wide circle, evidently looking for a horse, and had eventually located Rogan's bay with next to no trouble. Rogan gazed at the hoofprints left by his mount, and judged that Calder would gain a start of many hours on him. He went back to the house to find Weedon leading in two saddle mounts. The deputy grinned ruefully at Rogan.

'These are our mounts, Rogan. I'll ride out shortly and pick up a couple of the horses we chased out of the corral last night. I'll be back by the time you've eaten.'

Rogan nodded and went into the house. He found Carter cooking, and sat down to a good breakfast. When he had eaten he confronted Kroll.

'I've heard tell there's a robbers' roost somewhere out here in the Territory, Kroll.' Rogan broached the subject uppermost in his mind. 'It's said to be run by a hardcase named Jake Yaris.'

'If there is I ain't heard of it,' Kroll replied. 'I don't know nothin'.'

Rogan gave up, aware that he would learn nothing. He heard the sound of hoofs outside and peered through a window to see Weedon returning and leading two horses. He hurried outside, impatient to hit the trail.

'I caught these two down by the creek over there,' Weedon said. 'Take your pick. I guess you'll want to be making tracks, huh?'

Rogan nodded. He selected a black horse that looked more than half-decent and led it to the shack by the corral where he picked up a saddle and a bridle. When he was ready to leave he rode over to the house. Carter was on the porch, dragging Kroll to the other spare horse.

'I'll see you back in Fort Smith when I've got Calder again,' Rogan said.

'Sure thing!' Carter grinned. 'We'll be looking for you, Rogan. Ride easy, huh?'

'It's been a pleasure working with you,' Rogan continued, and held out his hand.

Carter shook hands and Rogan turned to Weedon.

'Don't take any wooden nickels,' Weedon said with a grin.

Rogan nodded and mounted the black horse, which cavorted spiritedly until he brought it under control. He sent the animal across the yard at an easy lope, intending to return to the spot where his bay had been hobbled to take up Calder's trail, but the blasting roar of Weedon's shotgun shattered the early morning silence and harsh echoes fled across the range.

Shocked, Rogan twisted in his saddle, reaching for his pistol as he did so, and a burst of pistol-fire crashed loudly as he spotted five riders appearing from behind the shack by the corral. He barely had the time to see that one of them was Jed Calder before he was deluged in a volley of crackling slugs.

5

Rogan hurled himself sideways out of the saddle as slugs crackled around him. He hit the ground hard as the black staggered and then fell heavily, squealing in agony. Rogan crawled desperately to avoid being rolled on by the stricken animal. He heard Weedon's shotgun fire again and squirmed around in the dust as he lifted his pistol into the aim. He could hear slugs thudding into the black and ducked low behind it as he waited for the lethal storm of lead to ease.

Hoofs hammered the hard ground and Rogan pushed himself up to observe. He saw at a glance that Carter was down on the porch with Kroll beside him. The deputy marshal was triggering his pistol at the attacking riders. Charlie Weedon was lying on the ground just in front of the porch, his shotgun discarded, his body lying unnaturally still.

Calder and two of the riders were galloping across the yard towards the spot where Rogan was lying. Their rapid shooting threw harsh echoes across the range. Rogan heard slugs smacking into the carcass of the black as he lifted his pistol and returned fire.

The foremost rider was swept out of his saddle by Rogan's first shot. Calder swung away immediately and headed for the front right corner of the house, shooting at Carter on the porch as he did so. He was followed closely by the surviving rider. Rogan drew a bead on Calder, allowed for the killer's rapid progress, and fired swiftly. He saw Calder jerk under the impact of the slug and sway in the saddle as he vanished around the corner, but he was gone from sight before Rogan could fire again. The second attacker rounded the corner and the sound of their departure faded.

A third rider continued to ride at

Rogan like a Confederate soldier charging at Bull Run, shooting desperately as he covered the intervening ground. Rogan shifted his aim, squeezed the trigger, and the man pitched sideways out of his saddle as the pistol recoiled against the heel of Rogan's hand. The attacker bounced in the dust before lying inert.

Carter was up on one knee, and Rogan looked towards the porch in time to see the last of the attackers falling from his horse. Gun smoke drifted across the yard. Rogan leapt up and ran to where a horse had halted. He sprang into its saddle, swung the animal to face the corner of the house and rode fast in pursuit of Calder and his companion, waving a hand to Carter in passing.

Rogan rounded the corner and a gun blasted instantly. He ducked and heard the whine of a slug passing his right ear. He dashed sweat from his forehead and saw Calder and his sidekick swinging around to flee. Fighting an impulse to shoot — he did not want to hit his bay which Calder was riding — Rogan took out after the two badmen, pushing his mount into its best speed.

He knew at the outset that he could not overhaul Calder. The bay was much faster than the average animal and could run for ever. But Rogan had no intention of letting the killer escape. He holstered his pistol and set himself to getting the best out of his mount.

Both fleeing men reined in at the top of a rise and turned to throw lead. Rogan saw Calder slide a Winchester out of the bay's saddle boot and rode hurriedly into cover as the killer sent a couple of rifle slugs at him. Rogan heard flying lead cut through twigs near his head. He saw the badmen going on again and rode out of cover to continue the chase.

Rogan sweated profusely as he followed. The killers were drawing ahead inexorably, despite his efforts to gain on them. The fleeing men hit a long incline and spurred their horses, sending the animals forward at a breakneck pace. Rogan watched them drawing away, his teeth clenched in frustration. He could feel hesitation in the horse he was riding, and was not surprised when it began to falter on the slope. He could see Calder ahead, now drawing away from his companion, and he itched to shoot the killer, but desisted.

Nearing the top of the slope, where it was steepest, Calder's companion was almost on the crest when Rogan saw him pitch sideways out of his saddle. The man hit the ground and lay inert while Calder spurred over the crest and disappeared. The horse, relieved of its burden, halted immediately and stood trembling on the crest. Rogan went forward quickly to find the badman lying face down and unconscious on the rough ground — the back of his shirt was soaked with blood.

Rogan dismounted and bent over the man. He had seen Calder jerk in the saddle as he made for the corner of the ranch house, and assumed that Carter had caught this one as he reached the corner. The man had taken a slug in the right shoulder blade and the bullet had dusted him both sides, for blood was seeping from an exit wound in the front of his shoulder.

The man groaned as Rogan turned him over. Rogan checked him and removed a pistol from his right holster. He ripped the man's shirt and used it to plug the entry and exit wounds. The wounded man remained unconscious during these ministrations and, when Rogan was satisfied he had stanched the bleeding, he hoisted the man face down across the saddle of the waiting horse and left the animal standing with trailing reins.

Rogan drew a Winchester from the man's saddle scabbard and checked the weapon. He reloaded the magazine to its full capacity and moved to the top of the rise, looking for Calder. The killer was riding fast into the distance and disappeared eventually over another ridge. Rogan mounted his horse and, leading the wounded man's animal, returned reluctantly to the Spooner ranch, his teeth clenched and his eyes narrowed as he considered the change in his fortunes.

Rafe Carter was sitting on the edge of the porch nursing a bullet wound in his left arm when Rogan arrived. Charlie Weedon was lying dead in the dust in front of the porch. Rogan dragged his prisoner off the saddle and stretched him out on the porch. Carter looked up at Rogan with lacklustre eyes. He had made an attempt to treat his wound but blood was oozing through the rough bandage he had applied.

'I hit that one as he went around the corner of the house,' Carter said through clenched teeth. 'There's no one else left alive around here. Kroll stopped a bullet that was meant for me and it killed him. Did you get Calder?'

'No. He got away, but I can trail him later.' Rogan stifled a sigh. 'He's riding my bay. I'll take a look at your wound before we start back to the wagon.'

'I'd like to bury Charlie before we pull out.' Carter groaned as he got to his feet. He glanced at the wounded bad man. 'Is he hit bad?'

'Bad enough, but I think he'll make it. I'm wondering who those four are and how Calder met up with them.'

'The Territory is crowded with badmen.' Carter shook his head. 'You don't have to ride back to the wagon with me, Rogan. Get after Calder and take him. I can handle this chore. I'll head back to the wagon with this prisoner and take him on to Fort Smith.'

Rogan nodded slowly as he considered the situation.

'I guess you're right,' he agreed. 'I need to get after Calder before his trail goes cold. I hit him before he reached the corner of the house and he might have to lie up if he's hurt bad. It's a chance I can't afford to miss. I'll dig a grave for Charlie before I go on.'

Carter moved to the unconscious badman, bent to examine him, and looked up at Rogan with sudden interest showing in his eyes.

'I've seen this galoot before,' he said eagerly. 'I don't know his name but a couple of years ago he was riding with a gang led by a thief named Jory Gillam. I'll take a look at the others we downed and see what we've got. See if you can stop my arm bleeding or I'll be in trouble before I can get back to the wagon.'

Rogan attended Carter's wound. He managed to stop the bleeding, and Carter sat on the edge of the porch and drank water from a canteen while fighting off an attack of shock. His face was pasty, his eyes narrowed and semi-glazed.

'You're not in a fit state to ride alone with a prisoner in your charge,' Rogan observed, shaking his head. 'I'll get you back to the wagon before going after Calder. That killer will keep. Sit here and rest while I dig a grave.'

Carter made no protest. He sat down again, leaned his back against a porch post and closed his eyes. Rogan went to the shack, found a long-handled sod buster, and dug a grave at the edge of the yard. They buried Charlie Weedon with the minimum of ritual. Rogan dragged the other dead men out of sight, and then prepared to ride out. He helped Carter into a saddle and put the badman face down across another horse, shaking his head as he did so.

'I don't think he'll survive the ride,' he judged, 'but he'll die anyway if we leave him here. It looks like he needs a doctor bad.'

'That's his hard luck,' Carter said unfeelingly. 'Let's get moving. The sooner we catch up with the wagon the better.'

They rode out at little more than a walk, and Rogan chafed impatiently at the situation in which he found himself. He needed to be on Calder's trail but contained his impatience and pushed on, halting for cold food at noon and then moving on a little faster during the long hot hours of the afternoon. Carter began to show signs of a fever as evening approached.

The badman was dead when Rogan checked him at sundown when he made another halt. Carter crawled into his blanket and slept until around midnight. Rogan sat motionless, unable to sleep, his thoughts intrusive, and he looked up when Carter moved suddenly.

'How you feeling?' Rogan asked.

'Much better now.' Carter got to his feet. 'Let's ride on, huh? I know this area pretty well, and we can make up a lot of time if we ride through the night.'

Rogan saddled their horses and they set out; neither man spoke during the hours of darkness and, when the sun came up, Rogan cooked breakfast on a small campfire and they drank coffee.

'I can go on alone from here,' Carter said when they were ready to ride again. 'You'd better get back on Calder's trail. Thanks for your help, Rogan. I hope you get your man.'

'If you're sure you'll be OK,' Rogan said doubtfully. 'I've lost so much time with Calder now that a little longer in catching up with him won't matter.'

Carter nodded, held out his hand, and said 'Good luck.'

Rogan shook hands and then swung into his saddle. He turned the horse and began to back-track to the Spooner ranch, aware that Calder now had many hours' start on him. He rode at a canter, and several hours passed before he reached the isolated ranch buildings. It was around the middle of the afternoon when he reined up to study the deserted spread. He was about to bypass it to head for the spot where he had last seen Calder when he spotted movement down in the yard and immediately rode into cover, hoping against hope that Calder had returned.

There were five horses in the corral, Rogan discovered. Two men were sitting on the porch and another was standing by the tackle shed with a rifle cradled in his arms. Rogan remained in concealment, watching the movements of the men, needing to know something about them before revealing his presence. When two men emerged from the house to stand on the porch talking, Rogan felt a strand of excitement dart through his breast, for one of the men was wearing a law star which glinted in the sunlight as he moved.

Rogan fetched his horse and swung into the saddle. He checked his pistol and eased it in its holster before riding openly into the ranch. The guard with the rifle covered him as he crossed the yard. Rogan kept his hands in view as he reined up to confront the four men on the porch. The man wearing the sheriff's star was big and capable-looking, in his forties, and wore a pistol on a sagging cartridge belt, the holster tied to his right thigh with a leather thong. His pale-blue eyes were like gimlets as he studied Rogan's approach.

'Howdy?' Rogan greeted. 'I spotted you from way out.'

'Who are you?' the sheriff demanded

brusquely. His gaze took on an even sharper look that was tinged with an edge of suspicion as he noted Rogan's hawklike appearance and hard manner.

'I'm Buck Rogan, deputy US marshal from Dodge City, on the trail of a killer named Jed Calder.'

'You got papers to prove that? I'm Sheriff Bob Hanton. We're looking for a bunch of robbers who hit the bank in Fort Smith. They headed in this direction but we lost their tracks about two miles back. I know that Spooner, who ranches here, is in cahoots with every badman who passes through, and I was hoping to find signs around here of the gang I want. But we found Spooner dead on a ridge a couple of miles from here, and there's no one else around, except some dead men by the shack over there.'

'I put them there yesterday,' Rogan said. 'I killed Spooner a few days ago.' He stepped down from his saddle as he explained the incidents that had occurred. When he mentioned meeting

Frank Shiloh and the law wagon and what had evolved thereafter, Hanton cursed mildly.

'Hell!' he said. 'I knew Frank Shiloh and his team were in this area.'

'Shiloh was murdered by the man I'm pursuing,' Rogan said. 'And Charlie Weedon was killed when Calder turned up here with four hardcases and took us by surprise. Those four are dead but Calder got away, and I need to get after him before he kills again.'

Rogan produced his papers and Hanton subjected them to a close scrutiny. The sheriff nodded when he returned them.

'Say, I've heard about you,' he said. 'I got a wire some days ago from Marshal Halfnight telling me about the attempted robbery at Fort Bradnum last week. Halfnight mentioned you — said he knew you in Dodge City. That was good work stopping that bank raid, Rogan, and I'm glad to make your acquaintance. Is there any way I can help you?'

'Only if you can tell me anything about a robbers' roost that's supposed to be out this way some place which is run by an outlaw named Jake Yaris. In Kansas we believe most of the lawlessness starts with the Yaris outfit down here.'

Hanton shook his head doubtfully. 'I've heard tell of such a place, but I don't know if there's any truth in it. I know plenty about Jake Yaris — thief and killer that he is. But I ain't met anyone who has set eyes on his hideout. Mebbe you're flogging a dead horse in that direction.'

'I've got to check it out.' Rogan shrugged. 'Who are the robbers you're looking for? Can you put names to them?'

'From the witness reports I've got, I reckon I'm looking for Bill Doolin and his gang. Doolin is said to be holed up out here in Indian Territory, probably at that hideout you mentioned, and Marshal Tilghman has spared no efforts lately to get him but without success.

Doolin has made a big reputation with a string of robberies and getting away with a lot of dough.'

'The only way to bust this set-up is to get an army of lawmen out here and make a clean sweep through the whole area,' Rogan observed, 'and someone has got to check out if there is a robbers' roost. There has been plenty of talk about it, and there's no smoke without fire.'

'It'll probably come to a stand-up battle with Yaris in the end,' Hanton agreed. 'I got my office in Fort Smith, and Judge Parker has made a good start against the badmen. He's got about two hundred special deputies ranging through here, and they're really cleaning up. Parker is the best thing that ever happened to Arkansas. There is no appeal against his judgments and he hangs most of the prisoners his lawmen arrest. So you killed Spooner and his outfit, huh? Give me the details and I'll make a report about it for the record when I get back to Fort Smith.'

Rogan explained about Mrs Miller and the freighters Hewitt and Garrett, and Hanton listened intently. When Rogan finished his narrative, Hanton jerked a thumb towards the house.

'Come inside and I'll take a statement from you. Grub is about ready, if you're hungry. It's getting a bit late in the day to start looking for tracks. We're staying here until morning. I've got my best tracker out at the moment, looking for sign. If you're gonna be searching around here for your man then watch out for Doolin and his bunch. If you fall in with them you won't live to talk about it. This is mighty dangerous territory for a lone lawman. I've had a number of undercover men venture through here, and they've never been seen again.'

'Thanks for the warning.' Rogan smiled grimly. 'My job is to take on bad men where ever I come across them. If I meet up with the Doolin gang they'll know they've been in a fight. But right now all I'm interested in is Jed Calder.'

The sound of approaching hoofs cut through the heavy silence hanging over the ranch and Rogan turned to see a rider coming in at a gallop. The guard had lifted his rifle at the sound, but lowered it as if recognizing the newcomer.

'That's Curly Preston,' Hanton observed. 'He's riding like his horse is on fire. I reckon he's found tracks. I hope so. I need to get on and settle the hash of whoever robbed the bank in Fort Smith.'

The rider brought his mount to a slithering halt in front of the porch and sprang out of his saddle in a cloud of rising dust. He was tall and lean, dressed in drab range clothes, and his black Stetson was pushed off his forehead to reveal a crop of yellow curly hair. He grinned widely as he stepped up on to the porch where Rogan and Hanton were standing.

'I got their trail again, Sheriff,' he reported. 'They blotted out all sign for at least a mile, but I rode around in a wide circle and cut across them where they stopped blotting. I followed them for a mile, and they're heading deeper into the Territory.'

'We'd better ride out now,' Hanton decided. 'I don't wanta lag too far behind them. There's grub inside, Rogan. Take what you want. I reckon you'll pick up Calder's trail in the morning, huh?'

'Yeah.' Rogan nodded. 'My horse needs to rest. I'll stay here tonight and hit the trail at sun-up.'

Hanton and his posse moved quickly, and in a few moments they were riding away from the ranch. Rogan watched them go, and a sense of loneliness gripped him as he took care of his horse and put it into a stall in the barn. He watered the animal and then fed it with a forkful of hay and some oats from a barrel standing just inside the door. Satisfied that the horse was comfortable, he returned to the house carrying his saddlebags and rifle, and entered the kitchen, where the smell of cooking food on the stove reminded him that he was ravenous.

After a meal, Rogan found the daylight fading and shadows appearing. He took his rifle and saddlebags and left the house. He led his horse from the barn and knee-hobbled it in dense brush at a safe distance from the ranch before bedding down beside it. Full darkness came as he unrolled his blankets, and he lay for a time watching the stars appearing in the dark velvet sky before sleep claimed him.

A faint crescent of the moon was high in the sky when the faint clop of hoofs alerted Rogan. He came awake instantly, gun in hand, and raised his head to listen intently. When he heard the sound again he slid out of his blankets and moved to the head of his horse, placing a hand over the animal's nostrils. He heard the movement of the approaching horse and followed its progress by the faint sounds it was making. Someone was riding into the ranch, and taking pains to ensure that he was not overheard.

Rogan guessed the time was well after midnight. He patted his horse and left it while he walked into the ranch. If he was lucky then the newcomer would be Jed Calder, still sneaking around like a preying coyote, but he was aware that the rider might be a scout for a gang of outlaws — perhaps Jake Yaris. Whoever was moving around, Rogan had to check him out. He closed in with relentless determination, making no sound as he followed the furtive sounds made by the unknown horse.

6

Rogan paused when he reached the front yard of the ranch. His eyes were accustomed to the shadows as he looked around for the mystery rider. He saw nothing, and was aware that a deadly silence hung over the spread. He assumed that the rider was watching the spread for signs of human presence, and he crouched patiently, content to wait until the newcomer satisfied himself that the place was uninhabited and moved again.

Minutes later Rogan heard the sound of hoofs to his right. He turned his head slowly and spotted the faint shadow of a horse crossing the yard. The rider had dismounted and was walking beside the animal — just an intangible movement in the night. Rogan waited patiently, his hand on the butt of his pistol. Horse and man were swallowed by the dense shadows around the porch and silence fell. An interminable time passed when nothing moved or sounded.

Rogan continued to wait, and minutes later he saw a dim light appear at the open doorway of the building. The newcomer had entered the house. Lamplight flared brightly, and then the door was closed. Rogan began to ease forward, intent on getting a look at the newcomer. He made no sound as he crossed the yard, and reached the side of the house without incident. He paused for a long time, looking around and listening intently, certain now that the man in the house was alone.

When he stepped on to the side of the porch the horse tethered at the front lifted its head and whickered. Rogan halted instantly, and clenched his teeth when the light in the house was extinguished. He moved against the wall, gun half-drawn, his eyes narrowed and his nerves taut. The silence was overwhelming.

The front door creaked slightly as it was opened cautiously. Rogan could see nothing and awaited developments, his breathing slow but his nerves leaping in anticipation of sudden action. He sensed rather than saw the man, and restrained his breathing, gripping his gun and bringing it slowly out of its holster.

'Damn you, hoss!' a hoarse voice whispered. 'You'd make a noise if you saw a jack rabbit. I'll attend to you after I've had my fill. Just stay quiet. There ain't anyone around here.'

The door closed again and Rogan heaved a silent sigh of relief. A moment later the lamp inside the house was relit. Rogan moved close to a window and risked a look at the man inside, who had turned to the stove. The man was dressed in dusty range clothes and looked as if he had travelled far. He was tall and lean, his face covered with a dark beard above which his nose protruded out of all proportion to his features.

Rogan moved away from the window, his thoughts racing. The man had approached the ranch and entered the house as if he had a right to be inside. Rogan did not think he was a stranger for he had arrived in the dark and seemed familiar with the layout. Aware that there was only one way of learning the man's business, Rogan drew his pistol and catfooted to the door.

He opened the door and lunged into the wide room, his movement startling the man, who swung around from the stove, his right hand dropping instinctively to the butt of his holstered gun.

'You don't need your gun,' Rogan said crisply. 'Just get your hands up and tell me your business.'

'Who in hell are you?' the man countered. 'You came busting in here like a tornado! You could have gotten yourself shot, moving around like that in the dark. Say, I ain't seen you around before. You must be a new hand. Where is Spooner and the outfit? I rode a long way to bring word from Jake Yaris, and found the place deserted.'

Rogan's eyes narrowed at the mention of Jake Yaris, and he thought of Spooner lying dead out on the range. So Spooner *had* been in cahoots with the outlaws! Rogan moistened his suddenly dry lips as a strand of excitement speared through him.

'Spooner took the outfit to Fort Smith to lift some dough from the bank there,' he bluffed. 'I was left here to watch the place, and I sure wanta know who you are, mister.'

'The handle is Dave Bridger. I ride with Yaris. How long have you been with Spooner?'

'Several weeks! I came into the Territory with Two-Finger Kroll and his bunch, herding stolen horses. I put some business Spooner's way and he gave me the chance to work with him.' Rogan realized that he had nothing to lose and everything to gain by bluffing, and if he could string Bridger along then so much the better. 'I've heard a lot about Jake Yaris,' he mused. 'He runs that robbers' roost I've heard about.'

Bridger chuckled. 'Everybody has heard about that place but no one knows where it is, except a few men who can be trusted. Who told you about it? Was it Kroll? Yaris trusts him, but Kroll is known for his loose lip. If too many folk get to know about the hideout it won't be long before the law starts taking an interest. When do you expect Spooner back?'

'He left only a few days ago so he won't get back inside of a week.'

'Heck! I can't hang around here that long. I gotta be making tracks back to Yaris. You can tell Spooner Yaris wants to talk to him. There's a real big job coming up in a couple of weeks and Yaris wants enough guns at his back to handle it. He needs Spooner's bunch to back him. Yaris trusts Spooner. They go back a long way and they've done a lot of jobs together. So tell Spooner soon as he gets back that the big boss wants to jabber with him.'

'Sure. I'll tell him. Take what you might need from here before you ride out. I've got to get back to watching the spread. There've been signs of lawmen prowling around recently.'

Bridger nodded. 'Thanks. I'll stay tonight and pull out at first light. You're watching this place real well. Tell Spooner to get out to Yaris soon as he can. Maybe you better chase after him and give him the word. Yaris said this is a really big one, and Spooner should drop everything and rattle his hocks.'

'I can't leave the place,' Rogan shook his head. 'I got strict orders from Spooner, and it's more than my job is worth to go against them.'

He left the house and faded into the dense shadows to await a reaction from Bridger, but the man seemed content with the situation and remained in the house. Rogan went back to his camp and rolled himself in his blankets, but did not sleep. He lay looking at the stars until they faded and the first grey suspicion of dawn began to tinge the dark vault of the heavens.

Bridger rode out before the sun showed. Rogan heard the man's departure but did not see him in the shadows. He sat for long minutes after silence had returned, aware that he was faced with a difficult choice — he could follow Calder's trail or try to track Bridger to the Yaris hideout. When the sun showed on the distant horizon he was still contemplating his options.

The sun was clear of the horizon before Rogan left his camp. He watched the ranch for movement but saw nothing along the approaches. When he was satisfied that he was alone he rode into the yard to take care of his horse before going into the house to breakfast. He wasted no time and was in the saddle thirty minutes later, heading for the last place he had seen the fleeing Calder. His primary task was to bring the killer to justice and he would spare no effort to achieve that task. His thoughts were harsh as he continued.

He followed the tracks left by Calder

and reached the spot where he had last seen the killer. He cast around for prints, found them and went on determinedly. Calder was many hours ahead, but he had been wounded in their last shoot-out and Rogan had no idea just how badly the killer was hurt. With any luck the man would be unable to ride far, and might be close by, lying up like a wounded animal.

The tracks veered around in a wide circle and headed west. Rogan had no trouble following the trail left by his bay and settled himself to the onerous task of tracking the killer. He was not surprised when he discovered the tracks were heading back to Spooner's ranch, and when the sun had reached its zenith he found himself looking down on the deserted spread from a point beyond the corral.

Calder had camped in the brush just beyond the corral. Rogan dismounted in a flattened area and studied the ground. A ragged piece of white cloth, heavily bloodstained, lay half-hidden in the brush and Rogan studied it, aware that Calder must have sustained a serious wound.

Tracks led on from the site, and Rogan proceeded with some optimism. He followed with little difficulty, and was many miles from Spooner's ranch by the time the sun went down. He made camp and settled in his blankets in full darkness, containing his impatience until the sun showed next morning. When he went on he pushed the horse at a fast clip and moved through the wilderness, narrowed eyes watching the tenuous trail he was following.

Calder seemed to have some definite destination now and was heading deeper into the Territory. Rogan watched for signs of ambush as he continued. Calder knew the pursuit would continue, and if he was seriously hurt he would hunt cover like a coyote and try to murder his pursuer. Several times during the day Rogan turned aside from the trail and circled a particularly dangerous-looking piece of ground to avoid a possible shot from cover. It cost him some extra time, but he was still making good progress by the end of the day.

Three days passed while Rogan continued to follow the trail. Aware that Calder was not making fast progress, he was certain he would soon confront the man. He set out on the fourth day, buoyed up by the knowledge that he had closed the distance between them. It was around noon when he spotted a stream ahead, glinting through a stand of trees. Calder's tracks led straight into the thick cover, and Rogan halted to survey the scene.

His keen gaze soon picked out the stark lines of a wagon under the trees. There was no movement anywhere, and Rogan drew his pistol and checked it before moving in slowly. He could hear the sound of running water, but there was nothing moving under the trees and he closed in, alert to all possibilities.

As he drew nearer he saw that the wagon was in a small clearing, and two horses were hobbled nearby. The silence was overpowering. Rogan noted that the wagon did not have a cover on but a tarp was spread out and tied down over its load. He reined in and called loudly to announce his presence. As his voice echoed under the trees he spotted a saddle horse standing off to the left, recognized his bay, and threw himself sideways to the ground.

Rogan's pistol was in his hand as he covered the area. A deadly silence existed around the camp. He could smell wood smoke and the enticing aroma of cooked food, but nothing moved except the horses by the wagon. Rogan got to his feet and closed in, angling towards the wagon, his pistol levelled. He fully expected Calder to confront him suddenly with a blazing gun but there was no movement and he took his time checking out his surroundings.

He began to think that Calder had made his usual murderous visit upon some unsuspecting traveller, and expected to find dead folk in the camp. He neared the rear of the wagon and paused when he saw the muzzle of a Winchester poking out from under a corner of the tarp cover. There was a slight movement and he sidestepped quickly to get out of the line of fire. He cocked his pistol and his right index finger trembled on the trigger.

'Who's under the tarp?' he called. 'I can see you. Come on out, and leave the rifle lying. Be quick or I'll shoot.'

There was no response, but the rifle muzzle moved slightly. Then Rogan heard a young girl's voice cry out under the tarp. He frowned and moved quickly to the corner of the wagon. He grasped an edge of the tarp and twitched it aside to reveal a boy of around twelve and a girl a couple of years younger lying in a cavity in the load of household items in the wagon.

The boy raised his hands instantly and sat looking at Rogan with wide, fear-filled eyes. The girl stopped crying, lowered her head and covered her eyes with grimy hands. Rogan gazed at them in wonder, and drew a quick breath as he grasped the import of the scene.

'Who drives this wagon?' he asked, and had to repeat the question twice before the boy answered.

'Our pa, Charlie Tolliver, drove it from Ohio.' The youngster spoke in a harsh flat tone. 'We were on our way to Guthrie where our Uncle Bill Tolliver owns the livery barn. A man came up on us yesterday, riding that bay. He shot Pa in the back and took our saddle horse because the bay's got a swollen joint. The man searched Pa's body and stole all our money. He said he'd kill us if we didn't stay quiet, and we've been here ever since.'

'Are you gonna shoot us?' The girl lifted her head and gazed at Rogan with shock in her gaze, blue eyes glistening with tears.

'No.' Rogan smiled sadly as he shook his head and unaccustomed emotion clawed at his throat. 'I won't hurt you. You got nothing to worry about now.

Where is your pa? Are you sure he's dead?'

'He's dead all right.' The boy nodded grimly. 'That killer shot him twice in the back as Pa bent over the fire to pour a cup of coffee for him.'

'Tell me what the man looked like,' Rogan urged.

'He was not very big — about half the size of Pa — and he smiled all the time, but his eyes were hard. He wore two pistols, and was fast, real fast when he drew one of them. Pa never knew what hit him.' The boy had difficulty in remaining unemotional His voice had a catch in it and he sniffed and wiped his eyes on his sleeve as he relived the shooting.

'I know the man you're talking about,' Rogan said. 'I'm hunting him. He's a real bad man and has killed other folk. That bay is my horse which the killer stole from me. What's your name, boy?'

'Henry Tolliver and this is my sister Aggie. I'm glad you showed up, mister.

I guess we got to go on to Guthrie and tell Uncle Bill what happened to Pa, but I don't know the way, and Pa is lying over there covered with a tarp. I reckon I should have buried him, but it didn't seem right, putting him in a hole and throwing earth on him.'

'Where's your ma?' Rogan asked.

'She died last year. That's why we're going to Guthrie. Pa said we'd start a new life there. But it ain't gonna happen. It's all over now. We got no hope left.'

Rogan fell silent, his mind flitting over the situation. His instinct was to get after Calder immediately and put an end to his killing spree, but he knew he could not leave these children alone in the wilderness. It was out of the question. He would have to suspend his pursuit of Calder and take these kids to safety.

'I'm riding to Guthrie,' he said. 'You can travel with me. I'll get you to your Uncle Bill.'

The relief of the two youngsters was

evident as they climbed out of the wagon. Henry Tolliver was tall and lean, looking as if he was accustomed to hard work, and he went off immediately to check on the two horses. Aggie stood looking at Rogan. She appeared hesitant, undecided what to do and he smiled at her.

'What chores do you handle around the camp?' he asked. 'Can you cook?'

'I sure can. Ma taught me before she died.'

'I could do with some coffee,' Rogan hinted, 'and maybe some hot food. Would you handle that while I take a look at my bay?'

Aggie nodded and went to the smouldering campfire. Rogan watched the two youngsters for a moment, shaking his head as he considered Calder's merciless actions, aware that if the killer had not escaped from the law wagon these two kids would not now be orphans.

Rogan went to where the bay was standing and found the animal favouring its left foreleg. The fetlock was slightly swollen and felt inflamed to Rogan's touch. He made a fuss of the animal, which snuffled in recognition, and led it to the stream where he bathed the fetlock in cold water He searched his saddlebags, found a cloth, soaked it in cold water and wrapped it around the fetlock.

He checked the body of Charlie Tolliver and found the man had been shot twice in the back. Rogan went to the wagon, where Henry Tolliver stood with the rifle in his hands, looking around as if he expected Jed Calder to spring out of cover at him.

'That killer is long gone now,' Rogan said. 'Is there a sod-buster in the wagon? I'll dig a grave for your pa.'

Henry produced a spade and Rogan began to dig a hole beside the stream. The ground was soft and easy to work, and when the grave was deep enough Rogan went to the body. He searched the dead man's pockets, but Calder had taken everything of value. He wrapped the tarp around the corpse and carried it to the grave. Henry and Aggie stood by while Rogan said a few appropriate words. The girl began to cry and Henry led her away to the back of the wagon. Rogan busied himself filling in the grave, and afterwards flattened the fresh earth before placing some rocks on the mound.

Rogan ate a meal, and tried to get the kids to eat but both refused food. Then they set about breaking camp and, when the wagon was ready to roll, Rogan had one thing more to do.

'You said Calder rode out on your pa's saddle horse,' he said. 'Tell me about it.'

'It's a chestnut. Pa was proud of that horse. It could run like the wind and stay for ever. The killer took it — he couldn't ride the bay any more.'

'Show me exactly where he rode off,' Rogan directed. 'I need to see the chestnut's tracks so I can remember them.'

'Over here.' Henry led the way to the stream. 'He gave the chestnut a drink before crossing the stream and heading west.'

They walked to the stream and Henry located hoof prints in some soft ground. He squatted and looked closely at the prints before gazing up at Rogan.

'These belong to the chestnut,' he said. 'I know them well.'

Rogan dropped to one knee and subjected the prints to a close scrutiny, looking for characteristics that would enable him to recognize them should he see them again. He noted that the left front shoe had about half an inch missing from the inner end. He followed the tracks beyond the stream to check the direction Calder had taken.

'Are you a lawman?' Henry asked. 'You said you were hunting that killer.'

'I've been on his trail all the way from Kansas,' Rogan replied, 'and he's killed a lot of folks between here and Dodge City. I'll come back to pick up his trail when I've seen you to Guthrie. Can you drive the wagon?'

'Sure. I can handle the team.'

'Then get moving. I'll tie the bay behind and ride my other horse alongside. It looks like your pa was following a regular trail which probably leads to Guthrie. Follow those wheel tracks over yonder while I scout ahead to get my bearings.'

They broke camp. Henry helped Aggie on to the high driving seat and took up the reins. He proved to be expert with the team, and as soon as the wagon was moving in the right direction Rogan rode away at a canter to scout the trail ahead. He looked back, saw the wagon following steadily, and heaved a sigh as he pushed on. He rode for a couple of miles, checking wheel tracks in the ground, which formed a well-used trail, and guessed that all he had to do was follow them to reach Guthrie.

He dismissed Jed Calder from the forefront of his mind. He could not be in two places at once, and he had to see Henry and Aggie safe before he would be at liberty to resume his duty. Calder would have to wait, and Rogan was sure of one thing. The killer would not escape the law, even if it took years to catch him.

Rogan was about to return to the wagon but decided to surmount a nearby rise to check the trail ahead. He reined in on the crest of the high ground to scan the wilderness and was surprised to see a cabin in the middle distance situated close to the trail. A large corral to one side contained at least a dozen horses, and Rogan grinned at the sight. The place looked like a relay station, which meant a stage coach ran regularly through here to Guthrie. He glanced back the way he had come and saw the wagon in the distance, coming along steadily. Movement attracted his gaze beyond the wagon and he noted a cloud of rapidly moving dust approaching which could only mark the presence of a stage coach.

At that moment the sound of a shot echoed through the wilderness. Rogan's head jerked around as he searched for the source of the disturbance and he saw six riders reining up in front of the cabin and what looked like the body of a man lying on the ground in front of the building.

One of the riders pulled a rifle from his saddle boot and lifted it to his shoulder. Rogan ducked and rode off the crest of the rise, for the rifle was pointing at him from a distance of about 200 yards. He was barely down in cover when a bullet crackled ominously past his head.

7

Rogan slid out of his saddle and pulled his Winchester from its scabbard. He scrambled back to the crest and bellied down to look at the cabin. A rider was coming fast towards him. Rogan jacked a cartridge into his breech and waited. He saw the five riders back at the cabin dismount and lead their horses around to the back of the building out of view. Then he returned his attention to the approaching rider. It seemed that he had ridden into the middle of a projected stage hold-up. He clenched his teeth as he considered that this particular area was a real hotbed of robbers and killers.

The approaching rider came straight for Rogan's position carrying a rifle across his saddle horn. His intention was obvious. Rogan glanced along his rifle barrel and lined up his sights on the man. The rider reined in suddenly and lifted his Winchester to his right shoulder. Rogan ducked as the man fired, and heard the whine of the slug passing closely over his head. Satisfied as to the man's intentions, Rogan squinted through his sights, aimed off a fraction to allow for the breeze, and squeezed his trigger.

The flat crack of the rifle threw sullen echoes across the wilderness. Rogan opened his right eye and watched the rider pitch out of his saddle. He slid back off the crest, stood up and went to his horse. He regained his saddle and looked towards the wagon. Henry, having heard the shooting, had stopped the team and was sitting with his rifle in his hands. Rogan held up his hand palm outwards to warn the boy to remain where he was and, when Henry replied with a wave, Rogan turned his horse towards the cabin.

The five men were standing in front of the cabin, weapons in their hands. Rogan found cover and swung in a circle to approach them from a different direction. In the background he could hear the pounding hoofs of the stagecoach team and even the raucous voice of the driver as he urged his horses on at their best speed. Rogan pushed his mount, wanting to be in a good position to intervene in the robbery by the time the coach arrived.

He was only fifty yards from the left front corner of the cabin when the stagecoach came clattering along the trail. It swerved to halt in a cloud of dust in front of the building. The five men, spaced out in a semicircle, moved forward with levelled guns, and Rogan lifted his rifle. He fired at the nearest man in the line and saw him spin and drop to the ground. The other four started shooting at the coach, and the blasting crash of the guard's shotgun sounded heavily, punctuated by the booming reports of Colt fire.

The guard on the stage dropped his shotgun immediately and pitched off the high seat. The driver had dropped his reins and was desperately working a pistol. Gun smoke drifted around the coach. Rogan shifted his aim and fired again, his sights lined up on a second robber. The man jerked under the impact of the slug, then dropped to his knees before falling forward on his face. The three remaining men turned to run towards the left corner of the cabin, intent on gaining cover, and Rogan snapped shots at them as they were on the point of disappearing from sight. He thought he had missed, but two men suddenly broke their rapid strides and fell to the ground. The sole survivor vanished from sight, and a moment later Rogan saw him astride his horse and fleeing fast.

Rogan urged his horse forward, rifle in his left hand. He slid the Winchester into his saddle boot as he neared the coach and lifted a hand to the stage driver, who was covering him with a pistol as he closed in. The driver was an old man, probably in his fifties, short and fleshy, with a battered black

Stetson pushed back off his wrinkled forehead. He lowered his pistol as Rogan reined in beside the dead guard.

'Thanks for your help, mister,' the driver called. 'We were in real trouble until you homed in. I never saw shooting like yours. Where did you come from? Them robbers sure made a big mistake taking you on.'

'You passed a wagon back on the trail.' Rogan swung out of his saddle. 'I'm taking a couple of youngsters to Guthrie. Their pa was murdered a couple of days ago.'

'I saw them when I came by. I wondered why a young 'un was driving that team.'

Rogan bent over the inert guard and found him to be dead with a widening stain of blood on his shirtfront. The driver jumped down from his high perch and bent over the guard.

'Pete's dead!' He spoke in a voice laced with shocked disbelief. 'Only a couple of minutes ago he said he was looking forward to reaching Guthrie

146

because his wife was cooking something up for their twentieth anniversary.'

'I'll check on the others.' Rogan shook his head. 'There were six robbers. They shot a man in front of the cabin before you arrived.'

'That'll be Joe Harmony. His wife is out here with him. I'd better see if she's all right.'

'I don't think the robbers got inside the cabin,' Rogan said.

He checked the inert figures lying in the dust. One robber was breathing his last and the others were dead, mute testimony to Rogan's fast, accurate shooting. The driver spoke to passengers in the coach, telling them to remain inside the vehicle, then he hurried to the door of the cabin, calling a woman's name as he did so.

'Martha, where are you? You can come on out now. It's all over. Hurry it up. Pete is down in the dust.'

Rogan approached Joe Harmony, lying in front of the cabin, and was relieved to find him alive. Harmony had been shot through the right shoulder and he was semi-conscious. Rogan dropped to one knee beside the man, who opened his eyes as Rogan touched him.

'You'll be OK, Joe,' Rogan said quietly. 'The robbery failed. Just lie still and we'll get you fixed up.'

'My wife,' Harmony muttered. 'Is she OK?'

Rogan looked towards the cabin door as the driver reappeared with a woman behind him. They came to where Harmony was lying and Rogan backed off.

'I'm Hank Arlen,' the driver said, confronting Rogan. 'The stage company sure owes you a vote of thanks for what you did here. I'll need your name for my report, and if you're going on to Guthrie there'll be a big welcome waiting for you when you get there.'

Rogan shook his head. 'I'm Buck Rogan. Forget about what happened here. There's something you can do for me.'

'Anything,' Arlen said eagerly. 'You just name it.'

'I'm trailing a killer but I'm saddled with those two kids in the wagon back there. They need to get to their uncle, Bill Tolliver, who owns the livery barn in Guthrie. Will you see them there safely? Their wagon can remain here until Bill Tolliver arranges for it to be collected.'

'So you're a lawman, huh?' Arlen grinned. 'Sure thing! Those kids will be safe with me. They can ride in the coach. I got a couple of female passengers who will take care of them.'

'Thanks.' Rogan turned away. 'I'll fetch that wagon in fast as I can. You're the answer to my prayers.'

'Don't hurry,' Arlen said, grinning. 'After what happened here it won't matter if I'm late getting to Guthrie. I hope you get your man, Rogan.'

'I'll get him,' Rogan retorted.

He returned to his horse and cantered back along the trail to where the wagon was waiting. Henry Tolliver was on the driving seat of the wagon, a rifle across his knees, and his face showed the seriousness of his thoughts as Rogan reached him.

'I heard all that shooting,' Henry said. 'Was it Pa's killer?'

'No. Shake up the horses, Henry, and I'll tell you about it as we ride. There's a relay station just ahead and a gang tried to rob the stagecoach which passed you. I happened to be in the right place at the right time and managed to put a stop to the robbery.'

He explained his arrangements with the coach driver as they went on, and Henry shook his head.

'I don't like the idea of leaving the wagon behind,' he said doubtfully.

Rogan grimaced. 'It will be safe at the way station, and your uncle can arrange for it to be collected when he knows what's happened. You've got to think of Aggie's safety. She should be more important to you than a wagon.'

'I guess you're right.' Henry lapsed into silence until they reached the way station.

Hank Arlen was ready to roll when Rogan approached him. He had hitched a fresh team of horses to the coach.

'Let's get the youngsters aboard,' he said. 'I got to be splitting the breeze now. I'll have to take Joe and Martha into Guthrie. The stage company will send another man out here until Joe recovers from his wound. Pull the wagon over beside the cabin and unhitch the team. The horses will be OK in the corral until a relief man arrives. There's a stream runs through a corner of the corral so the horses can drink when they want, and they can help themselves to hay from a stack inside the corral.'

In a few moments Henry and Aggie were climbing into the stagecoach. They peered out at Rogan as Arlen shook his reins and cracked his whip. The coach lurched forward and Rogan lifted a hand in farewell. Henry waved in return, but Aggie merely gazed unblink-ingly at Rogan until the coach had almost vanished in a swirl of dust before she acknowledged their parting with a tentative wave.

When the coach had disappeared, Rogan turned his thoughts to duty. He had to get back on Jed Calder's trail, but first he needed to check on the robber who had fled when the shooting started. He swung into his saddle and rode around the cabin to look for tracks. He soon spotted the prints which had been left by the fleeing rider. The man had galloped off into the nearest cover and Rogan followed cautiously.

He crossed a stream, found more prints, and continued. The tracks crossed the stream again and headed north along the bank where the brush was thickest. Brush grew almost shoul-der high around Rogan as he trailed the running horse. He ducked to get under the low branch of a stunted oak and descended an undulating slope to a bend in the stream. At that moment a pistol hammered twice. He heard the crackle of closely passing lead and dived out of his saddle to hit the ground hard on his left shoulder. He listened to the fading echoes of the shots.

Gun in hand, Rogan pushed himself to one knee and searched the saddle-bags on the horse for extra shells for the pistol. He found a box of .45 cartridges and filled his pockets before looking around. He was pleased his quarry had not quit the area, and strained his ears to pick up unnatural sounds. He heard a horse cropping foliage somewhere ahead and eased towards the sound, moving a step at a time, his big pistol cocked and ready. When he spotted a brown horse ahead he recognized it as the animal the fleeing robber had used to get away from the cabin. He crouched as he began a slow circle of the area, intent on getting behind the robber. Silence was heavy around him, but each movement he made seemed amplified and he knew his quarry could hear his approach.

He heard his own mount begin to feed, and the sound of it attracted a further shot from ahead. Rogan pinpointed its position by a thin trace of gun smoke drifting away. He closed in, wondering why the robber had turned to fight and, when he trod on a twig which snapped loudly in the silence, another slug crackled through the brush. It whined past his left shoulder in blind flight.

Rogan suddenly spotted a man's head and shoulders in a gap in the brush. Traces of blood showed dully on his left shoulder, and he realized why the robber had fled from the cabin. He had taken a slug in that first swift interchange of shots! Rogan covered the man as he prepared to move in, but as he pushed forward a fusillade of shots hammered through the silence and a hail of slugs cut and slashed into the surrounding brush. Rogan threw himself full length and rolled down the slope until he reached the bank of the stream.

He slid his feet over the bank and eased into the gurgling water. A sustained burst of shooting enveloped him and he ducked low, wondering what was happening. There had to be at least six men up there lying in ambush, and Rogan cursed himself for assuming there was only one man ahead and for not taking all the usual precautions before moving in.

Voices began calling out as the unknown men above shouted instructions and warnings to each other. Horses crashed in the thick brush and Rogan lifted his pistol and waited for his first sight of the opposition. He was lying in a slight depression in the bank of the stream but it was not good cover, and he realized that he needed to be working his way out of the trap instead of planning an uneven fight against this bunch, whoever they were, for they seemed to hold all the aces in this grim game.

He could hear the ominous sounds of horses closing in all around his position and flattened against the bank to reduce his target area. He tried to pull brush around and over his body, but the noise he made attracted more shots, and slugs whined and snarled around him in a lethal storm. He lay motionless until the shooting dwindled away.

Rogan slid deeper into the water and crouched under the bank. The current of the stream had cut away part of the bank to leave a narrow overhang and he thrust his body into its cover like a burrowing animal, clenching his teeth determinedly as he forced himself to lie still and await developments. Hoofs thudded on the hard ground and a rider neared his cover, searching the area intently.

A pistol blasted and the bullet struck the bank only a foot or so from Rogan's position but he did not move, sensing that the rider was attempting to get him to betray his position with a return shot. He lay motionless, breathing slowly through his mouth while sweat ran down his forehead and stung his eyes. The horse crackled through undergrowth on its way past Rogan's position, the rider urging it constantly. The man called out that there was no sign of an interloper.

'He's down there somewhere, Taffler,' an authoritative voice replied hoarsely. 'Get into the stream and look around. Mason said it is the guy who killed most of the gang when the stagecoach arrived at the relay station. We've got to nail him. He's likely to be a lawman and I want him dead. We've spotted his horse back here, so he's afoot, and with any luck you can take care of him.'

'One man ain't gonna make much difference to our plans,' the rider retorted. 'Send someone else down here to give me a hand, Jake. The brush is too thick to check out easily. I need some help. This guy knows what he's doing. Send Eke in here. He's got a nose like a bloodhound.'

Rogan wiped sweat from his face

with his left hand. His pistol was covering the dense brush from which the rider's voice emanated. The man was several yards to the left now, and trying to force his horse into the stream judging by the noise he was making. Rogan eased himself into a sitting position and peered around. He spotted the rider in the act of entering the stream and holstered his pistol as the man turned and came back towards the spot where Rogan was positioned. The newcomer was a big man, broad-shouldered, sharp-faced, with a straggly brown beard adorning his lower face. He held a pistol in his right hand which was poised ready for action.

Rogan eased in under the branch of a stunted oak which was low over the water. He watched the rider splashing his way closer. The stream was belly-high to the horse and the current was fierce where it negotiated the bend. Rogan did not want to use his gun. He waited until the horse almost stood upon him before surging upright from under the thick branch and lunging at the rider. His left hand secured a grip on the man's gun hand as he sledged his right fist against an unprotected jaw. He dragged the man out of the saddle and hit him again to subdue him. Then he drew his pistol and stuck the muzzle under the man's chin.

The man was semi-conscious. Rogan thrust his head under the water and held it there for several moments before lifting him clear of the surface. The man spluttered and coughed. Rogan supported him with his left hand, and the threat of the levelled pistol kept him subdued. He looked up at Rogan, who motioned for him to remain silent.

'Hey, Taylor, what are you doin' down there?' a voice called from above. 'Are you taking a bath?'

Several men laughed hoarsely, and Rogan grinned despite the gravity of the situation, but did not relax his hold on the prisoner. The man gazed at him with fear in his dark eyes.

'Just stay quiet,' Rogan warned, 'and

you might still be alive when this is over. Tell me who you are and who that bunch is up there.'

'I'm Frank Taylor. The boss man up there is Jake Yaris, and you ain't got a prayer of getting out of this alive. Better give up now and save yourself a load of trouble.'

'No dice! Where do you and this bunch hide out when you're not out on the rampage?'

'Now you're asking! Yaris would have my life if I told you! You're gonna have to do this the hard way, mister. If you want the answer to that question you'll have to go up there and ask Yaris himself.'

Rogan's thoughts were already leaping ahead of the situation and he knew instinctively that it was time to get away and then swing around to trail the gang when it moved out.

A burst of shooting erupted from above and bullets raked the area. Rogan ducked, dragging Taylor down with him, and the muzzle of his Colt remained jammed against his prisoner's neck. They lay motionless until the lethal storm ceased.

'OK, you men,' Jake Yaris ordered. 'Three of you get down in that stream and put an end to this. Make it quick. I want to get on to the Spooner ranch.'

The sound of several horses crashing through the brush warned Rogan that his position was becoming untenable. He stood up and slammed the barrel of his pistol against Taylor's head, catching the man just above the left ear. Taylor gasped, and Rogan struck again. Taylor sagged limply and Rogan dragged him to the bank and thrust him up out of the water. He turned, grasped the reins of Taylor's horse, and was leading the animal upstream when the guns above opened fire yet again to rake the area just behind his position. He kept moving, teeth clenched in anticipation of stopping a slug, but gradually eased away from the danger area to leave the shooting down-stream.

When he was clear, Rogan swung

into the saddle and put his spurs to the animal's flanks. The horse lunged forward, splashing mightily, and Rogan kept it going although it seemed determined to disobey. The ground on either side of the stream rose up and he was forced to continue upstream. The horse was making a lot of noise, but silence was impossible. Rogan gritted his teeth and continued. He glanced back over his shoulder when he heard another fusillade of shots.

The shooting was directed at a point lower down the stream, and Rogan covered at least half a mile before the left-hand bank became lower and he was able to dismount and climb out of the water, tugging the now amenable horse behind him. The brush was dense and he remounted on dry ground and swung away from the stream as fast as the horse could travel but did not ride far. He circled and returned to the stream, crossed it, and slowed to move in on the spot where Yaris and his bunch had ambushed him.

He could hear horses splashing in the stream but stunted trees and vegetation hid them from his view. He did not fire, for he had heard Yaris say he wanted to head for the Spooner ranch. He dismounted, left the horse in dense cover and sneaked forward to observe the gang. He paused when he saw riders gathering on the bank and waited in cover until the hardcases began to move away downstream. He fetched his horse and followed at a distance, guided by the sounds they were making, until Yaris called them together.

'OK. Stop wasting time and let's get out of here. We got things to do. Did anyone see Taylor down there?'

There were negative replies, and Rogan heard crashing sounds as the gang withdrew from the stream and assembled on the bank. He saw a big man sitting the saddle on a magnificent black horse and realized he was looking at Jake Yaris. The gang leader was big and powerful, with a fleshy face and a reddish beard that covered only his chin and jawline. He was holding a Winchester across his saddle horn, and kept shouting instructions to his men. His gaze was never still, always checking his surroundings, and he seemed to have the stark awareness of a predatory mountain lion.

'Get a move on!' Yaris yelled. 'We've wasted too much time as it is. Millican, you ride drag, but stay here and watch our back trail for a spell. I got a hunch that lawman will swing round and follow us. Take him alive if you can, but don't let him get away if he shows up. Nail him good.'

Rogan watched the bunch ride off, five hardcases who set a fast pace through the brush. Millican, left to watch their back trail, dismounted behind a knoll and hunkered down out of sight. Rogan began to close in immediately.

Rogan's ears were protesting against the shooting that had occurred. Pressure had built up in his head and he yawned to dispel it. He left the horse in cover, drew his pistol, and circled around the knoll, moving slowly until he eventually found himself looking at Millican who was hunched on the knoll, watching his back trail.

The outlaw was small, stocky, with wide shoulders and big hands. He was holding a Winchester and seemed alert. Rogan studied him for some moments, noting his alertness, and then decided his course of action. He walked forward to the knoll with his pistol levelled. The outlaw whirled around when Rogan deliberately stepped on a twig which snapped loudly in the overpowering silence. His mouth gaped at the sight of Rogan's powerful figure and he instinctively swung the muzzle of his Winchester in Rogan's direction.

'Drop the rifle,' Rogan ordered.

Millican paused for the merest second. The muzzle of his rifle was still pointing skywards. Shock stained his face in an almost comical expression as he gazed into the black muzzle of

Rogan's levelled gun. For an interminable moment he was undecided what to do, but eventually he sighed heavily, released his hold on the rifle and raised his hands.

'Step away from the rifle and get your hands up higher,' Rogan commanded in a harsh tone.

Millican obeyed, his expression showing disbelief at the way he had been surprised.

'Where did you come from?' he demanded. 'I never heard a damn thing. Who in hell are you, mister?'

'Never mind that! I'll do the talking. Just answer my questions. How come your bunch happened to be around when the robbers tried to hold up that stagecoach?'

Millican shrugged. He moistened his lips, still badly shaken by Rogan's unexpected appearance.

'It was planned like that,' he said at length. 'The law has been getting stronger around here for months and Yaris won't take any chances. We were

166

covering against something going wrong, and you proved Yaris right. Mason said you turned up out of the blue and shot the hell out of the gang. They never had a chance against you. How did you know the robbery was gonna take place?'

'I told you I'll ask the questions. Give me truthful answers or otherwise keep your mouth shut.' Rogan moved in and searched his prisoner. He had decided to leave the man afoot when he went after the rest of the gang. He turned to look at the prisoner's horse, and at that moment was struck on the head from behind. It was as if a mountain had fallen on him. One moment he was doing his duty and the next he was crumpling unconscious into the dust.

8

Rogan's first awareness when he opened his eyes was a crushing pain in his head which pulsated with each heartbeat. He closed his eyes quickly. The sun was shining directly into his face and he lifted his right arm to shield his eyes from its dazzling glare. For some moments he wondered what had happened, and then a harsh voice spoke nearby.

'Ike, he's coming round. What are we gonna do with him?'

'Take him with us of course. Yaris will want to question him. Are you sure he's the guy who did the shooting at the relay station, Taylor?'

'It's him OK, and he got the better of me in the stream. The skunk stole my horse too! I got a lot to settle with him. I oughta finish him off here and now. He's a real tough galoot. I never saw shooting like his. He put slugs into everyone standing around the coach. We sure can't take any chances with him.'

'Get him up on his feet then. We've got to get after the others. They're heading for the Spooner place. Come on, let's get moving.'

Rogan's shoulders were grasped and he was shaken violently.

'Wake up. We got places to go. Get on your feet!'

Rogan opened his eyes as he was dragged upright. For an instant his senses swirled. He leaned heavily on the man lifting him until his head cleared, then he glanced around. Taylor was holding him while Millican stood only feet away, rifle in his hands, watching closely. Rogan noted that he was covered from Millican's rifle by Taylor standing between them and instantly slammed his right fist into Taylor's stomach.

Taylor wilted like a tree struck by lightning. Rogan grasped him as Millican began to move and thrust him bodily into Millican, whose rifle fired a shot as he inadvertently squeezed the trigger. Taylor yelled in agony and dropped instantly, falling against Millican. Rogan staggered as his senses reeled, but he lunged forward to fall upon both men. He reached desperately around the apparently lifeless Taylor and secured a grip on Millican's rifle as he rolled clear of the two men, taking the rifle with him.

But Millican retained a hold on the Winchester and dragged himself to his feet as he cleared Taylor. Rogan grasped Millican and held him close, the rifle pinned between their bodies. Millican stood a head shorter than Rogan but was immensely strong, which was readily apparent when his thick arms encompassed Rogan's upper body in a powerful bear hug. Rogan lifted a knee and slammed it into Millican's groin. The man groaned and fell away.

Rogan staggered back. He tried to bring the rifle to bear but Millican came up off the ground like a wildcat and hurled himself forward, a tight grin on his lips. His left fist swung in a short arc and his heavy knuckles crashed against Rogan's jaw. Rogan had never been hit so hard. Lights flashed in his brain and he began to sag, but managed to duck the next blow and hung on to the smaller man, shaking his head to clear it of the effects of the punch.

Millican tried to get loose from Rogan's grasp. His left hand grasped the barrel of the rifle and he exerted tremendous strength to keep the weapon from being used against him. Rogan was dimly aware of Millican's heavy shoulders and powerful arms. He wanted to stay at close quarters to minimize the solid punches which came at him with slogging power and hurt tremendously. Millican ripped the rifle out of Rogan's hand, but only to fling the weapon aside before slamming a flurry of heavy punches with his rocklike fists. The granitelike knuckles came at Rogan as if they were driven by the pistons of a steam locomotive.

Every punch sent pain through Rogan's body and shook him to the core. He gave ground as a red mist slipped before his gaze but there was no respite. Millican was obviously above average in fist-fighting and Rogan began to suspect that he was on a hiding to nothing. His ribs felt as if they were being broken by the rain of blows which hammered him, and those punches he managed to block with his arms hurt as if he was being beaten with a sledge hammer. His ears became filled with an ominous whistling sound and his jaw began to ache ferociously but there was no let-up. Rogan fell backwards under the torrent of blows and lost his balance completely.

He was only dimly aware of his shoulders striking the ground and Millican coming at him with an upraised foot. Rogan flung himself aside as the boot came in and it merely grazed his chin instead of kicking him senseless. Millican overbalanced and sprawled on the ground. Rogan was filled with desperate strength which he summoned up from deep within. He jerked his aching body up on to his knees and managed to get to his feet before Millican recovered. He raised his aching arms to protect himself and loosed a left-hand punch as Millican rushed him again.

Rogan managed to get his timing right and his bunched knuckles thudded against Millican's jaw. He followed with a looping right that smacked against the other side of Millican's chin. To his surprise and relief Millican dropped to his knees like a poleaxed steer. Rogan staggered, almost fell, but recovered and stepped forward to kick Millican in the head. Millican flopped forward and lay inert, breathing heavily through his gaping mouth.

Rogan straightened, filled with overwhelming relief, and forced himself upright. His upper body was aching and his strength had fled under the punishment he had received. He looked around, and almost fell as he bent over Millican to snatch a pistol from the man's holster. He staggered thankfully back out of distance, having a healthy respect for Millican's prowess with his fists, and moved to where Taylor was lying. He saw that Taylor was dead, a rifle bullet in the centre of his chest, and he returned his attention to Millican, who was beginning to stir.

The sudden and rapid pounding of many hoofs suddenly became apparent and Rogan swung around to face the approaching sound. Half a dozen riders were coming in fast and Rogan lifted his pistol, fearing Yaris and his bunch had returned. Then he saw a glinting law badge on the shirt front of the leading rider and heaved a long sigh of relief when he recognized Sheriff Hanton. The posse was raising dust, and swung into a circle around Rogan, their guns drawn and levelled.

'It's Rogan,' Hanton said in some surprise. 'We heard a helluva lot of shooting a short time ago and figured we had got lucky. So what happened here?'

'Am I glad to see you!' Rogan swayed as he straightened. He was aching in every muscle of his tortured body. His face felt bruised and swollen and he could feel blood dripping from his right eyebrow. He explained the situation and Hanton straightened in his saddle.

'We ain't seen hide or hair of any badman since we left you at the Spooner place,' he said. 'It looks like you've had all the luck, Rogan. Do you feel able to ride? If so get up on a horse and we'll head for Spooner's ranch. I've heard a lot about Jake Yaris, and I'd like to come up with him before we ride back to Fort Smith. One of you men put some cuffs on the prisoner and keep an eye on him. Make it quick. We better light out fast.'

Rogan staggered to where he had left Taylor's horse and swung wearily into the saddle. Millican was cuffed and pushed into a saddle and the posse set out at a fast pace. Rogan stifled a groan as he was jolted, for every movement sent pain coursing through his bruised body, but his head cleared by degrees although his ears continued to sing from the effects of the punches he had taken to his head. He fought against his weakness as they continued.

'So you stopped the stage from being robbed,' Hanton commented when they halted later for a break.

Rogan supplied the sheriff with details, and Hanton shook his head when he learned of Jed Calder's latest murder spree.

'It's about time you put that killer where he belongs,' he mused. 'If we have any luck at Spooner's then I'll ride with you for a spell and see if we can't nail Calder. I reckon there's only one way to stop him, and that's with a bullet where he can't digest it.'

'He's sure having a big run of luck,' Rogan mused, 'but that will come to an end when we've settled Yaris.'

They continued, and Hanton sent a man ahead to watch for ambush. The tracks of Yaris and his bunch showed plainly on the rough ground, and Rogan began to entertain hopes that the posse would soon overhaul the gang, but when the sun went down they had not set eyes on a living soul.

'We'll keep on,' Hanton decided. 'I know this area well and if we get to Spooner's place before dawn we might catch Yaris unawares. Stay close, men. We're going to go for broke. We need to have some success under our belts when we ride back to Fort Smith. I reckon Yaris will know all about the bank robbers we've been after, so let's move on and see if we can't get something good out of this venture.'

Rogan was pleased by Hanton's determination. The posse remained in a tight group as they rode through the night. A thin sliver of the moon showed in the east and stars brightened in the dark velvet texture of the high and wide sky. Hours passed monotonously, and the posse made regular halts to rest their mounts. Rogan had no idea where they were and relied on the sheriff's local knowledge to get them to the Spooner ranch.

Grey streaks were beginning to appear in the blackness overhead when Hanton eventually reined in and stepped down from his saddle. He patted his horse as he looked around. A faint breeze was blowing into their faces as they dismounted. Rogan trailed his reins, wondering exactly where they were.

'Spooner's place is just over that rise in front of us,' Hanton informed the posse. 'From here on in nobody makes any noise. Just settle down while I scout ahead with the marshal to see if Yaris and his bunch spent the night here. If they are here we will surround the place and take them at first light.'

Rogan accompanied the sheriff and they moved forward on foot, ascending a rise to its crest, where they bellied down and gazed at the indistinct shapes of the buildings in the middle distance.

'There it is,' Hanton observed with

some satisfaction. 'Spooner's ranch! I don't think we should ride closer; they might hear our approach. I reckon to lead our mounts into a gully nearer the ranch and then move in on foot. How many men do you reckon are with Yaris?'

'Five at least,' Rogan replied. 'If we get into position and wait for them to come out into the open we might have a chance of nailing them all.'

'That's how I figure it.' Hanton nodded. 'OK, I'll bring the posse up and we'll get to it.'

Rogan remained on the crest while the sheriff moved back. The ranch was silent and still; looking ghostly in the greying light of approaching dawn. A strand of excitement began to unwind in Rogan's breast. He had begun to think that he would fail in all parts of his mission. Calder had escaped him and Yaris and the big hideout seemed to be a rumour without substance, but if Yaris and his men were here then there was a very good chance of an unexpected success.

A thin red-gold line had appeared in the even darkness of the sky over to the east when Hanton returned with the posse, all leading their horses. Rogan took his reins from the sheriff and led his horse as they set off down the slope towards the ranch, the sheriff walking slightly ahead. After some distance they finally entered a deep gully on the left side of the house. Hanton left a man with the horses to watch the prisoner and the rest of the posse followed the sheriff and Rogan as they moved in silently. Rogan was relieved when he heard a horse stamp in the corral and, by narrowing his eyes, made out the shapes of several horses confined there.

He pointed out the fact to the sheriff and Hanton nodded grimly.

'It looks like we've got them,' he replied in a harsh whisper.

The five possemen hunkered down in cover in positions where they could watch the yard and the corral and waited in total silence for the sun to show above the horizon. Daylight came imperceptibly with features emerging slowly from the deep gloom. Rogan looked for a guard but saw no movement anywhere around the ghostly yard. He grasped his gun and waited patiently for the sun to show on the horizon. The enveloping silence was heavy, like the inside of a cave.

'Someone is moving to the left of the house,' one of the possemen hissed, and all eyes swung in that direction.

Rogan saw the figure of a man standing at the lefthand corner of the building, and a little knot of excitement arose in his throat. He tightened his grip on his pistol. A tip of the sun appeared above the eastern horizon and the first long fingers of yellow brilliance stabbed across the wild landscape. Range of vision increased rapidly and Rogan blinked to clear his sight.

'I can see a wagon over at the side of the house,' someone reported. 'It looks like one of those law wagons used by the deputies from Fort Smith.'

'The hell you say!' Hanton eased up into a crouch and went scurrying to the left for a better look.

Rogan clenched his teeth and waited stolidly, fearing the worst — the badmen were not here. He saw Hanton straighten up suddenly and walk out into the open to confront the guard over by the house, who stiffened at his movement and lifted his Winchester to his shoulder.

'I recognize that guard,' Hanton said. 'It's Rube Smith, one of Judge Parker's deputies. Put your guns away and show yourselves, men.'

Rogan scrambled up along with the posse and they walked across the yard towards the suspicious deputy.

'Sheriff,' Smith called in surprise. 'What in hell are you doing, sneaking around like a bunch of criminals? Don't you know you could get shot, moving in like that?'

'Howdy, Rube? I was expecting to find a bunch of badmen holed up here; Jake Yaris and some of his boys.'

'There's nobody here except half a dozen deputies,' Smith replied. 'We came out from Fort Smith on the scout, and ran into Frank Shiloh's group on its way back to headquarters. They got a good haul of prisoners, but Shiloh was killed, and so were some of the others in his group. We reckoned to look around here before pushing on, and got here late yesterday afternoon, but we ain't seen hide or hair of anyone, until you showed up.'

Hanton shook his head slowly as he looked at Rogan. 'What do you think happened?' he asked.

Rogan suppressed a sigh. 'I guess we should have halted at dusk last night and waited for dawn to follow their tracks,' he replied. 'It looks like we'll have to back-track to find the answer to your question. I had a feeling before the sun came up that this was working out far too easy. I didn't think Yaris could be taken like this.'

'We'll grab some breakfast here and then ride back to where we last saw their tracks,' Hanton decided. 'I'm not giving up yet. That crooked bunch halted somewhere for the night and we must have passed them in the dark. Heck, they could still ride in here like a flock of pigeons coming home to roost. We better hide all signs of our presence until we're ready to ride out.'

Rogan swallowed his disappointment. They took their horses around to the rear of the house while the guard went inside to inform the rest of his crew of the posse's arrival. Hanton led the way into the house through the back door, and shook hands with a tall, powerful man whom he introduced to Rogan as Joe Crisp.

'So you're Rogan, huh?' Crisp said. 'I heard all about you from Shiloh's men. They reckon you can fight your weight in wildcats! Did you get that killer you were after?'

'Not yet.' Rogan shook his head. 'I was sidetracked by a coach hold-up, and then ran into Jake Yaris and some of his bunch. I heard Yaris say they were heading for this place, but they must have turned off during the night, or they might turn up this morning.'

'You need to hide your wagon, Joe,' Hanton said. 'We spotted it, and if Yaris does turn up he'll take flight if he spots it.'

Crisp gave orders and his five deputies moved quickly to obey. Rogan contained his impatience as the tired possemen settled down to rest. They ate breakfast, but Hanton was in no hurry to move out.

'We'd better rest our mounts,' he said when Rogan pressed him to go on. 'We might have a long chase ahead if Yaris has turned off somewhere, and we don't wanta spoil our chances if he turns up here after all. I don't reckon a few hours will make much difference.'

'I'll ride out now.' Rogan tried to curb his impatience but failed. 'I can trail back to where we last saw the gang's tracks and follow them from there.'

'OK.' Hanton nodded. 'We'll follow you later.'

Rogan went out back to collect his horse, and was chagrined to find the animal lame in its right foreleg. It was the horse he had taken in the stream from Taylor. Joe Crisp had followed him out of the house.

'There are a couple of spare horses in the corral,' Crisp said. 'They've got Spooner's brand on them, but he ain't gonna worry if you borrow one. You put him and his crew out of business, huh?'

'He won't rob anyone else, that's for sure,' Rogan replied.

He led the lame horse around to the corral where Crisp's men were catching their horses and found two animals wearing a Big S brand. He roped one of them, a capable-looking sorrel, switched his gear to it and then departed, moving swiftly through the bright morning back along the trail the posse had left during their night ride.

Relief filled Rogan when he hit the open trail. He was feeling easier this morning, although he ached in muscles he had not been aware existed in his powerful body and his left eye was swollen and sore. Ike Millican certainly knew a thing or two about fist-fighting, he thought ruefully.

It was noon by the time he had retraced the trail back to where he had last seen the tracks left by Jake Yaris and his men. He spent a long time walking around studying them in order to impress individual prints in his mind. He estimated six horses were in the outlaw party and remounted the sorrel to continue. He soon found that Yaris had turned away from his original intention of riding to the Spooner ranch; the tracks heading south-west instead of east.

Rogan pushed along at a fast clip, his thoughts ranging back over his past exploits. He wondered where Jed Calder was at that moment, and whether he would ever catch up with the cold-blooded killer. He did not like to think that Calder was still robbing and murdering innocent folk.

At noon he halted to rest the sorrel, but his impatience was such he could not delay long, and was soon back in the saddle to resume the trail. The nature of the terrain changed imperceptibly as he progressed and he eventually found himself riding over rocky ground which made tracking difficult. He was forced to slow considerably, and chafed at losing time, but the hoofprints before him were his only link with the outlaws.

On reaching the crest of a rise Rogan reined in quickly when he spotted a small herd of cattle being pushed along from his left across the direction he was taking. He rode back beyond the crest and dismounted to check out the four riders around the herd. They were moving the cattle at a fast pace and Rogan suspected they were rustlers. He was tempted to brace them, but the odds of four to one were too great at the moment and he needed to stay on the trail he was following.

He remained in cover until the herd

had disappeared behind a ridge to his right. The streamers of dust raised by the trampling hoofs of the steers drifted away and he continued, casting around for horse tracks after crossing the broad ribbon of flattened ground left by the cattle. It took him some considerable time to pick up Yaris's tracks again, and then he went on.

The sun was a long way over in the western half of the sky and shadows were filling the undulations of the ground when Rogan spotted a cluster of ranch buildings beside a wide, glittering creek. He reined in and considered his position. He could see the horse tracks left by Yaris and his men heading towards the ranch, and wondered if he had come upon yet another dishonest rancher who owed allegiance to the local badmen. The sun was going down now and vision was becoming poor as he gazed ahead.

He decided to move in closer and watch for signs of Yaris. He dismounted to lead his horse and walked to stretch his own legs, keeping under cover where he could. There were men moving around the yard of the ranch and they seemed to be carrying out normal chores. A trio of riders suddenly appeared from the back of the house and rode off to the south, moving at a canter and not looking left or right as they progressed.

Rogan halted and trailed his reins. He could see the faint tracks he had been following heading directly into the ranch yard. He knew it was dangerous to skulk around in this country but did not want to confront Yaris and his gang if the badmen were still here. He preferred to follow them and pick his own time and place for a showdown; he wished the posse had travelled from Spooner's ranch with him.

He observed the ranch from a distance but close enough to make out fading details and watch points. He saw a guard wandering around the yard, rifle in hand, and guessed he would get a hot reception if he showed himself.

Were Yaris and his bunch still at the spread? Rogan knew he had to find out and, pushed by impatience, eased back to where he had left his horse. He mounted and rode in a wide circle around the ranch, looking for signs of the gang leaving.

Night had almost settled in but he spotted where a bunch of riders had ridden out of the rear of the ranch. Rogan dismounted and checked the prints, nodding his satisfaction when he recognized them as being those he was following. They were fairly fresh, and headed north. Rogan swung into his saddle, turned the sorrel in the same direction to take up the trail again, thinking that he would clear the ranch and then make camp until morning. Then he caught a glimpse of a shadowy rider coming out of the ranch. Taken by surprise by the man's unexpected appearance, Rogan had no time to conceal himself. He sat his mount as the rider, having spotted his presence, came forward at a canter to confront him.

Rogan dropped his right hand to the butt of his gun and waited for the man to arrive. It was almost too dark now to make out details. The man was suspicious, for his right elbow was bent and he was grasping the butt of his holstered pistol.

'Who are you?' the man challenged. 'Speak up quick or you'll collect a slug.'

Rogan suffered a pang of pure shock as he heard the voice, for he recognized it immediately. The man was Jeff Calder, the killer whose trail he had followed tenaciously all the way down from Kansas!

9

Calder's right elbow jerked as he drew
his gun and Rogan moved as if
controlled by the same brain impulse,
his pistol lifting swiftly and smoothly
from its holster. He eared back the
hammer with his thumb before the
weapon was levelled, and then time
seemed to stand still for one heart-
stopping second. Calder was fast on the
draw, Rogan knew, and he brought all
his gun skill into play. He triggered a
blasting shot that was capped a split
second later by the report of Calder's
pistol; the two detonations so close
together they rolled into one fury of
raucous sound.

Rogan's bullet smashed into the killer
even as Calder fired, and the impact of
the heavy slug threw off Calder's shot
almost as it left his muzzle. The
spasmodic jerk of Calder's body was

sufficient to deflect his aim and Rogan felt the sorrel shudder as the bullet thudded the animal. Calder reined his horse away and galloped off into the darkness as a series of echoes fled across the darkened range. Rogan kicked his feet out of his stirrups as the sorrel pitched heavily to the ground, his vision temporarily dazzled by the muzzle flames which erupted from both guns. He sprang away from his horse before it could roll on him and staggered almost blindly as he raised his gun for a second shot at Calder.

But there was only the sound of the killer's horse fleeing into the shadows. Rogan could see nothing. The pounding hoofs faded to a faint drumming sound before ceasing entirely, and Rogan stood helpless in the night, unable to pursue his man.

Rogan bent over his horse to find the animal dead. He drew his rifle from the saddle boot and then slung his saddlebags over his left shoulder. He was afoot and had no choice but to visit the nearby ranch. He looked around, picked out the direction he wanted, and started walking quickly. Impatience flared through him because he was so close to Calder yet helpless to continue the chase.

The shots had attracted attention, Rogan soon discovered, for three men, one carrying a storm lantern, appeared from the ranch house and came towards him as he walked around the corral. All three men were armed. They halted some yards from Rogan, their weapons levelled at him.

'Who are you,' the foremost demanded. 'What was that shooting about?'

'Someone shot my horse from under me,' Rogan replied, thinking it better to keep his identity secret. 'I don't know who he was but he rode out of here a few minutes ago.'

'He just up and shot at you?' asked the man with the lantern.

'That's right. He never said a word; just pulled his gun and triggered it.'

'And he didn't hit you?'

'I was a mite faster than him,' Rogan replied. 'I tagged him and he rode off.'

'Then you're a lucky man, mister. Jed Calder ain't usually on the receiving end.'

'Does he work here?' Rogan demanded.

'Nope. I wouldn't give him a job if he paid me! He's a bad-tempered man at the best of times and too quick on the trigger for my liking. He dropped by for some food and to rest his horse, and that's all the help I'll give him. You must have surprised him out there. He's touchy, and would shoot before asking questions. Are you hurt?'

'No. He fired one shot which killed my horse.'

'Well, you'd better come to the house and we'll see what we can do for you. I'm Art Marlowe. I rent this place from the Indians. I have to be friendly to anyone who rides through because in this country you never know who is gonna show up. The week before last Bill Doolin and his gang stopped by, and this afternoon Jake Yaris and some of his boys looked in, but they don't cause any trouble so long as we mind our own business. We also get a lot of deputy marshals through here. They're trying to clean up the Territory. I don't take sides, and I find that's the best policy. If I try to draw a line anywhere I could find myself in bad trouble.'

'Thanks.' Rogan was not taken in by Marlowe's apparent friendliness, sensing tacit hostility in an inflection of his voice and too much eagerness to explain the situation. 'Maybe you can let me borrow a horse.'

'Are you looking for a riding job?' Marlowe asked.

'No. I'm in another business.' Rogan said no more and Marlowe did not press the point.

'You'll certainly need a horse to get to wherever you're going,' Marlowe mused. 'I feel responsible for what happened to you because Calder was leaving here, so I'll fix you up with a mount.'

'I'll write you a note for the price of a

horse — say twenty dollars,' Rogan said flatly. 'It will be payable by the governor's office in Kansas.'

'So you're a lawman!' Marlowe's tone sharpened.

'I'm Buck Rogan, Deputy Marshal. I'm in a hurry to take out after Calder.'

'Can you prove you're who you say you are?' Marlowe persisted.

Rogan produced his law badge and stuck it under Marlowe's nose. The rancher lifted his lamp high in order to inspect the glittering shield-shaped badge which had a small silver star at its centre.

'Looks mighty impressive,' Marlowe observed. 'OK, Marshal, we'll do what we can to help you. Nick, throw a loop on that black in the corral and bring it out here. Do you wanta come into the house for some grub, Marshal? You're welcome to whatever I've got.'

'No thanks. I need to get moving.' Rogan was keen to get away from the ranch. 'Hold the lamp up and I'll write you a note.'

'You can't track Calder in the dark,' Marlowe observed. 'You can rest up here until sun-up if you like.'

'That's kind of you but I have to be going. Thanks for your help.' Rogan opened a saddlebag and produced some writing paper. He scribbled a receipt which would be honoured when presented to the law office in Dodge City and handed it to Marlowe. 'See you around,' he added.

'Think nothing of it.' Marlowe showed his teeth in a grin. 'So long!'

Rogan took the black horse when it was led out of the corral and departed, leading the animal back to where his horse was lying dead. He felt a prickling sensation between his shoulder blades as he turned his back on Marlowe and the two men, but moved off into the shadows without incident. He could have done with a night's rest but did not trust Marlowe sufficiently to stay at the ranch. He preferred the cover of darkness to give him some protection. In this country it seemed that every man's hand was against the law.

He removed the saddle from the dead horse, prepared the black for travel, and felt easier when he had put distance between himself and the ranch. He rode in the direction Calder had taken but did not ride far in case the killer had turned off. He found a spot in a jumble of rocks and made camp, unwilling to proceed further until daylight arrived.

He unrolled his blankets and used his saddle to fashion a dummy figure. He took a pair of moccasins from a saddlebag, removed his boots and stuck them under the blanket to further the illusion that he was asleep. He left the black knee-hobbled and took his rifle to move off a few yards to a vantage point from which he could cover the campsite. He settled down behind a rock and tried to make himself comfortable.

He sat hunched over, dozing from time to time, but his ears were strained for the slightest unnatural noise. Several times he jerked into readiness and lifted his rifle while he looked around into the shadows, but nothing stirred in the night except small animals going about their nocturnal business. He managed to sleep for a couple of hours before dawn and was fully alert when the sky turned grey and his range of vision increased imperceptibly. He remained motionless, watching the shadows, his rifle ready in his capable hands.

The grey half-light of approaching dawn was deceptive. A chill wind whistled through the rocks and Rogan felt the need of some hot coffee but remained in his cramped position, watching the approaches to his camp. As the sun came up he began to think he had misjudged Marlowe, and was on the point of stirring to make breakfast when a rifle cracked sharply and a shot echoed.

Rogan saw the flash of the weapon and heard the thud of the bullet as it ploughed into his saddle under the humped blanket. A second shot was fired and the blanket twitched. Rogan clenched his teeth, thankful for his suspicion of Marlowe. He would be dead right now if he had not taken precautions.

He awaited developments, and moments later two men on foot appeared from a gully and came into the camp. They were several yards apart and held levelled rifles. Rogan lifted his Winchester and covered them, waiting patiently as they approached. One of the men reached the humped blanket and twitched it aside. He cursed and jumped back at sight of the saddle, swung around and lifted his rifle to cover his surroundings.

'He's not in the blankets,' the man yelled.

Rogan shot him in the chest and swung the muzzle of his rifle towards the second man, who started running back to the nearest cover. Rogan fired again and the man fell, to lie inert on the ground. Rogan jacked a fresh cartridge into his breech and waited while echoes fled to the horizon. He continued to watch his surroundings, but his instincts advised him that the two men were alone. He slid back out of his position and circled the camp on foot, studying the apparently empty landscape, especially in the direction of the distant ranch. There was no sign of movement anywhere.

Rogan broke camp and prepared to travel. He cast around for Calder's tracks, moving in a half-circle until he came eventually upon some hoofprints which looked fresh enough to have been made by Calder during the night. He decided to follow them, and checked his back trail again before heading out.

He had covered about two miles in the light of the new day when he spotted a horse standing with trailing reins at the foot of a rough outcrop of copper-coloured rocks which were jumbled in haphazard fashion to a height of many feet. The horse was standing forlornly, its head lowered and its eyes closed. Rogan reined aside into a gully and drew his rifle as he dismounted. He left the black with a rock placed on its trailing reins to prevent it running back to Marlowe's ranch and moved forward to study the apparently abandoned horse and the great pile of rocks.

Rogan crouched behind a rock and scanned the rocky barrier, looking for the glint of sunlight on metal and any movement which would betray the presence of an ambusher. He assumed that Calder had been hit hard and could ride no further, so had holed up and was waiting for possible pursuit. It was possible the man had reached this spot before expiring from his wound, but Rogan would not take any chances. He had a great deal of respect for Calder's ability with a gun and stayed low while he considered the situation.

The sound of approaching hoofs alerted Rogan to possible danger from another source and he turned around to see four riders approaching from the direction of Marlowe's ranch. Easing back into the rocks for better cover,

Rogan prepared for action, certain that Marlowe's men had found the bodies of the two men who had tried to kill him and were tracking him with the grim intention of finishing the job which had failed.

The riders spotted the horse standing near the rocks and halted to talk about the situation. Rogan watched them intently, certain that one of them was Art Marlowe. From what he had seen of the rancher in the night he had gained an impression that the man was big and powerfully built, with a fleshy face, and a man of similar appearance was giving orders now to the other riders. Two of them turned their mounts and rode off to circle around the rocks. Rogan stayed low, his rifle ready, his eyes narrowed against the dazzling sunlight.

Marlowe came forward with his sidekick. They did not find Rogan's horse in the gully and reined up near the rocks only a dozen feet from the spot where Rogan crouched.

'Is that Calder's horse?' Marlowe demanded.

'It sure looks like it,' his companion replied. 'What's he doing holed up here? You'd think he'd keep going until he was clear.'

'That marshal said he shot Calder, so it's likely that killer has reached the end of his rope.' Marlowe glanced around, his eyes showing bleakness.

'So where is the marshal? He killed Palmer and Thompson. The black's prints showed he was at the camp back there, and his tracks came in this direction. He could be lying up some place, watching us and fixing to shoot us. There are too many lawmen hunting around the Territory these days.'

'We need to find him and finish him off,' Marlowe said grimly. He looked around, then put a hand to his mouth and yelled, 'Calder, where in hell are you? What are you doing here? There's a marshal on your trail. You better get to hell out, if you are able.'

Rogan waited but there was no reply

from Calder. Marlowe shook his head.

'Get down, Mike, and take a look through those rocks. Calder might be dead in there, and he could be loaded with dough. He said he'd had some good pickings in the past two weeks. We better grab it before that marshal shows up and takes everything.'

Mike dismounted and moved to ascend the rocks. He had barely started to climb when a pistol boomed and gun smoke drifted from higher up. Mike twisted and uttered a screech as he tumbled back to ground level. Marlowe pulled his pistol and waved it.

'What in hell are you shooting at us for, Calder?' he demanded. 'We're the only friends you've got around here. Are you hurt? Is that why you've holed up?'

'Get away from me, Marlowe,' Calder replied without exposing himself. 'You and your crew are stinking buzzards, and you'd strip me to the bone if I let you get up here. I ain't hurt so bad that I can't gut-shoot anyone who tries it on with me. You better pull out before I cut loose. I'll pull out when the sun goes down.'

'That marshal is around somewhere,' Marlowe warned.

Calder laughed echoingly. 'That buzzard has been after me for weeks and he ain't got me yet. Now get out of here.'

'All right! I'm going.' Marlowe dismounted, went to where his sidekick was lying and bent over him. 'Heck, you didn't have to kill Mike,' he complained. 'What for did you shoot him? I've been a good friend to you in the past, Calder, and this is the way you thank me.'

'I'll shoot you if you don't get the hell out!' Calder replied. He fired a shot that raised a spurt of dust beside Marlowe's right boot before screaming away over the gully where Rogan was crouching. Marlowe sprang into his saddle and rode off fast, calling for his crew to follow.

Rogan watched them cantering off in the direction of the ranch. He had spotted the puff of gun smoke from Calder's shot and slid along the gully in cover until he had eased in behind the killer's position. Calder had picked his spot well. He was unassailable from the front, and the way up to his position was difficult from any other direction. Rogan sweated as he scaled the rocks, taking his time in order to remain silent. He carried his rifle in his left hand, the long gun making his chore all the more difficult, but he clung to it tenaciously and slowly but surely ascended.

It took him half an hour of sweating exertion to reach the apex of the rocks, where he paused with his head just below the top to recoup his strength and his breath. Silence was heavy over the barren, copper-coloured rocks, and he did not underestimate Calder. The man was wounded but would be twice as dangerous in that condition.

When he was ready Rogan eased upward another foot until his eyes were above the rim rock. He saw an undulating stretch of rocks and studied the area with a keen scrutiny. Nothing moved in this elevated place, but his sharp gaze spotted a boot sticking out between two flat rocks ahead and to his right. The toe was pointing down, indicating that Calder was lying on his stomach, and Rogan estimated it was the spot from which Calder had killed Marlowe's man, Mike. He pushed himself to his feet and approached the spot slowly, his rifle at the ready.

As he moved in at an angle, Rogan saw a part of Calder's leg, and eased away to his right before making his final approach to the position. When he was able to see the whole of Calder's body lying in ambush, the sun glinting on the long barrel of the killer's deadly pistol, he closed in and halted only feet behind the man. Calder was lying motionless, as if already dead, his chin resting on a rock and his hands clasped around the pistol.

'Get your hands away from that gun, Calder, and don't turn round,' Rogan said loudly. 'I've got you covered and I'm just itching for an excuse to kill you.'

Calder jerked at the sound of the grim command but did not turn around. He lifted his hands away from his gun before turning his head to look up at his captor. Rogan saw an ashen face which seemed to carry the unmistakable signs of approaching death in its pallor. Calder forced a vicious grin. Rogan saw blood trickling from the killer's mouth.

'So it's you again!' Calder observed. 'Well, you don't have to kill me. You did for me last night and I've been carrying one of your slugs in my chest from that little fracas we had in Spooner's front yard the other day. I'm on the way out, mister, so you can hold your fire.'

'Get up,' Rogan ordered. 'Don't try anything or you'll make the trip to Hell head first.'

'Do you think I'd hole up here if I could move?' Calder grinned again. 'My strength has gone. I've been waiting for you to show up. I'm done for, and you won't be able to move me. Just let me die in peace. I know I ain't got long.'

Rogan leaned his rifle against a rock and bent over Calder, ready for any trick the killer might try, but Calder made no attempt to move. Rogan saw a lot of blood covering the rock on which the killer was lying. He snatched two pistols out of Calder's holsters and flung them away before securing a hold on the man's belts and lifting him bodily out of his position.

Calder groaned in agony as he was moved. Rogan settled him down on his back and made him as comfortable as possible. Calder closed his eyes. His chest palpitated and blood oozed steadily from the wound in its centre. Rogan frowned, wondering how the killer had managed to get away from Marlowe's ranch. He saw a dried patch of blood higher up on Calder's chest, and guessed it was where he had hit the man in Spooner's front yard.

Rogan opened Calder's shirt, and

shook his head when he saw the position of the bullet hole Calder had sustained during the night. Calder's eyes were closed. Rogan judged him to be on the point of death, and realized it would be useless to even try to save him. Calder opened his eyes.

'I guessed you'd get me when I couldn't kill you,' he said. 'Nothing I did could put you off my trail.'

'You're cashing in your chips, Calder,' Rogan said bluntly. 'Is there anything you want to tell me before you kick off?'

'The hell there is! Anything you don't know about me will go with me, but there's something I will tell you. I saw Jake Yaris at Marlowe's ranch yesterday and we had a falling out. I spent a lot of time at the big hideout with Yaris, and it cost me plenty, but yesterday he got to figuring I was through around here and warned me to quit. If he hadn't done that I wouldn't have met you in the night. Now I'm lying in the dust and the blame is down to Yaris. I heard him talking about hitting the bank in

Westville, Kansas, in ten days' time. There's a shipment of cattle money going in the bank there. It's a big job, so you can get up to Westville, catch him red-handed and finish him.'

'Is that on the level?' Rogan demanded.

'You got it straight from the horse's mouth.'

Calder slumped and seemed to stop breathing but his eyes flickered and he looked up at Rogan. When he grinned his mouth was lopsided and blood dribbled from between his lips. 'Go get Yaris and kill him, the dirty double-crosser!' he snarled. 'He wouldn't even let me back in his hideout until I was fit again.'

Before Rogan could reply Calder slumped and his boot-heels kicked spasmodically against obdurate rock. His hands clenched and he groaned as his eyes rolled. Rogan watched stolidly as the man stiffened before slumping. Calder exhaled slowly and seemingly relaxed into death.

Rogan straightened and looked around.

He felt tired, exhausted even, and could feel only relief that the long manhunt had come to its logical end. He could feel no sympathy or pity for a killer like Calder, who had murdered repeatedly on his flight from Dodge City, and experienced satisfaction that the man had passed on to the place where he had consigned so many of his victims.

Rogan shook his head and turned to depart. Yaris and his bunch were out there somewhere and he had to keep on until he came up with them. He caught a flicker of movement from a corner of his eye and hurled himself sideways as he returned his attention to Calder. The killer was not dead yet, and was lifting a small hideout gun from his waistband. There was a bloodstained grin on his thin lips as he swung the weapon to follow Rogan's instinctive movement.

The gun exploded and the bullet clipped the upturned brim of Rogan's Stetson. Rogan went down in a roll and came to rest on his belly, his big pistol in his right hand. He fired swiftly and saw dust fly from Calder's shirt as the half-inch chunk of lead smashed into the killer's heart. Calder relaxed instantly.

Rogan heaved himself to his feet. He covered the motionless body as he went forward, but his need for caution was no longer necessary. Jed Calder was dead.

'You were tricky to the last!' Rogan observed. 'And you sure had me fooled. You looked like you were dead, but I should have known better. You never gave up, you buzzard, and you nearly caught me on the wrong foot. But this time you are finished and good riddance.'

Rogan left the body lying in its lonely place and looked around for an easy way down to where he had left his horse, conscious of great relief. Calder was dead and now he could concentrate on Yaris.

He was about halfway down to the

ground when a gun cracked and a bullet smacked rock only an inch from his head. Rogan hurled himself sideways and fell into cover behind a rock as a second slug arrived. He was not hit, but had left some skin on sharp rock. He lay motionless in cover while a storm of bullets splattered around his position like lethal rain. After what seemed like a timeless period the shooting eased and then petered out. He raised his head to observe, wondering if Yaris and his gang had returned.

But Al Marlowe was sitting a horse in the back-ground while eight of his crew came forward to attack the rocks. Rogan lifted his rifle and jacked a cartridge into the breech. He watched several of the men open fire and heard their shots hammering against the rocks around him. Seeing that they meant business, he glanced along his sights and began to shoot rapidly. Gun smoke drifted, searing his throat.

He emptied three saddles in quick succession. The remainder of the riders turned tail and headed for the nearest cover. Rogan sent them on their way with a fusillade of shots which sent two more pitching out of their leather. Marlowe waved his arms and shouted orders, but was ignored. The survivors found cover well back from the rocks, and moments later they contented themselves with shooting at Rogan from a distance.

To Rogan it looked like a Mexican stand-off, and he waited to see what Marlowe would try next. The rancher had taken cover and, as the minutes ticked inexorably by, the shooting tailed off until an uneasy silence reigned. Nothing more happened until the surviving riders suddenly broke from cover, Marlowe among them, and galloped off in the direction of the distant ranch. Rogan watched them departing, his eyes narrowed. He finished his descent without further incident and entered the gully for his mount. He checked his weapons before riding out and then headed towards Marlowe's ranch. The rancher had proved he was crooked and would have to be dealt with.

10

Rogan saw no sign of Marlowe or the surviving members of his crew as he moved in the direction of the ranch. When he saw the roof of the ranch house from a distance he reined in, checked his weapons, and looked around for the best approach to Marlowe's position. He kept the horse to a walk when he went on, and his big pistol was clenched in his right hand, ready for action. He was cold inside, determined to clean up the small fry standing between him and the culmination of his duty.

He reached a spot which gave a view of the yard and his hard eyes took on a glint when he saw two men standing in front of the house with drawn guns. There was no sign of Marlowe but he did not doubt the crooked rancher was waiting under cover. He dismounted holstered his pistol and drew his Winchester from its boot. The metallic clicks which sounded as he cocked the weapon seemed loud in the strained silence. Tension gripped his throat as he crouched to lessen his target area. He began to close in.

A rifle cracked and echoes fled through space. Rogan heard a bullet pass the right side of his head and dropped flat, lifting his rifle to his shoulder. A puff of gun smoke was drifting away from one of the two men in front of the house. Rogan squinted along his sights, drew a bead on the man, and fired. The man threw down his rifle and pitched forward on to his face. His companion turned to dive through the open doorway of the house and Rogan sent a bullet after him which splintered the door post after passing through the man's left thigh.

Rogan got up and went forward. He heard glass shattering from a front window of the house and saw a rifle muzzle poke through the aperture. He fired three shots at the rifle in a lethal spray that sent more glass tinkling. The rifle fell out through the window. Rogan could guess what happened to the man.

He moved in closer, and was suddenly disturbed by the crackle of a spate of shots erupting from behind the house. More than a dozen shots were fired and echoes fled in a long string. Rogan paused, rifle at the ready, and heard the sound of hoofs thudding to his left. He turned his head, saw two riders appearing from cover at the edge of the yard, and swung to face the threat, ready to sell his life dearly.

One of the men waved a hand and pointed the muzzle of his rifle sky-wards, then came forward at a trot. Rogan recognized Sheriff Hanton. He lowered his rifle and got to his feet as he waited for the lawman to reach him.

'Rogan, we had the helluva chore keeping track of you from Spooner's ranch.' Hanton grinned as he slid from his saddle and faced Rogan. 'We heard shooting some time ago and closed in to check out the place. You appeared, and moved in before we were in position. That was mighty fine shooting. You don't waste much lead, huh?'

'I'm glad to see you, Sheriff,' Rogan responded. 'I was about to enter the house when I heard that shooting out back.'

'I sent some of the posse around to cover the rear.' Hanton was serious-faced. 'I've known for a long time that Marlowe is crooked, and could tell by your tracks back along the trail that you were heading here. It looks like you haven't left much for us to clean up on, huh?'

'I killed Calder earlier.' Rogan explained the incidents which had occurred since his arrival the previous evening. When he mentioned his run-in with Jake Yaris and his bunch Hanton's gaze sharpened.

'He was here yesterday?' the sheriff demanded. 'Wait a minute and I'll get Curly Preston to look for tracks. He did a good job trailing you, and if Yaris left a trail anywhere then we could be in business because Curly will sniff it out. I'm keen now on wiping out Yaris and his bunch.'

The rest of the posse appeared around a corner of the house, and Rogan saw Art Marlowe among them with metal cuffs on his wrists.

'I've waited a long time to catch Marlowe breaking the law.' Hanton said, 'and thanks to you, Rogan, I've got him dead to rights. Hey, Curly, come and have a talk with the marshal. He said Jake Yaris was here yesterday.'

Marlowe was sullen and disinclined to talk. Hanton questioned him on the whereabouts of Yaris and learned nothing.

'I saw Yaris at a stream a few miles from here,' Rogan said. 'His bunch tried to nail me but I fought them off. Yaris was astride a big sorrel. I recognized him from a dodger I've got. Now Calder is dead I'm free to follow up on Yaris.' He glanced at Marlowe, who was watching him intently.

'Where is Yaris hiding out?' he demanded.

Marlowe shook his head sullenly. 'I don't know. Yaris keeps his place secret. I ain't got any idea.'

'How many riders were in his gang?' Preston asked. 'I'll ride out and circle the spread. If Yaris left here yesterday then I'll pick up his tracks, you can bet.'

'There were four men with Yaris when I last saw him,' Rogan responded.

Preston swung into his saddle. 'I might be some time,' he said, and rode out of the yard.

Rogan watched the tracker cast about for prints. He was impatient to hit the trail, but needed to make some preparation before riding. He went for his horse and led the animal into Marlowe's barn, stripping off his gear before watering the animal. He fed it oats and hay and then went over to the house. Marlowe was seated on the ground outside the front door with a posse man standing guard over him. The smell of cooking food wafted out of the house, making Rogan realize that he was ravenous.

'We're gonna have to part company when we've had something to eat,' Hanton said when Rogan went into the kitchen. One of the posse men was supervising the cooking and Hanton was seated at a wooden table, watching what was going on. 'Much as I'd like to accompany you to get Yaris, I'll have to be getting back to Fort Smith, Rogan. If Yaris is gonna hit the bank in Westville in a couple of weeks then I've got to get word to the law department there and I can send a wire from Fort Smith.'

'If you can do that it will take a load off my mind,' Rogan observed. 'I could be riding around out here for weeks and not set eyes on Yaris. The alternative would be for me to make straight for Westville and set an ambush there, but there's a chance Yaris won't turn up.'

'I'll get back to Fort Smith without delay,' Hanton said. 'We've been out a long time now and the men are getting too tired to go on. I'd advise you to look for Yaris, and if you do come up with him don't lock horns with him. Get the lowdown on his hideout, and if he ain't going to Westville then you'd better come to Fort Smith for help. I'll have a big posse standing by should you bring the word, and we'll make a clean sweep right through here and settle this lawlessness once and for all.'

'Thanks.' Rogan nodded and smiled. 'I'll be riding out soon as I've had my fill of some of that grub on the stove.'

The possemen ate and prepared to move out. They had a long ride back to Fort Smith and Hanton was impatient to get on. Curly Preston returned from looking for tracks, and cantered into the yard, waving and calling,

'I've found some tracks that will interest you,' he called to Rogan. 'Come and take a look-see. Half a dozen riders pulled out of here about twelve hours ago and they've left a plain trail.'

Rogan walked across the yard and followed Preston to the west. They covered forty yards before Preston halted.

'They were moving pretty fast, judging by depth of their prints, so they've left a clear-cut trail,' Preston said. 'I'd like to ride with you and take a shot at Yaris, but I doubt Sheriff Hanton will let me side you, and I don't think you'll have any trouble tracking them.'

Rogan dropped to one knee to look at the tracks, and quickly spotted some prints which he knew intimately.

'See these?' He glanced up at the attentive Preston. 'My bay made these, and it was taken from the place where I had a run-in yesterday with the Yaris gang, so one of that outfit is riding it.'

'That's a good break.' Preston nodded. 'All you've got to do is trail your own horse, which couldn't be easier.'

They returned to the ranch. Hanton had his posse ready to ride out and ordered Preston to catch up after he had eaten. Rogan watched the party depart with Marlowe in their midst, and when Preston followed the posse a little later Rogan felt keenly the sense of loneliness which enveloped him. He stood in the yard and looked around, his thoughts beginning to turn on the immediate future, and felt the irresistible urge to push on and get to grips with Yaris and his bunch.

He fetched his horse and prepared to travel, but before he left the deserted ranch he took time out to check and clean his weapons. Then he rode out, picked up the trail Yaris and his men had left and settled to the task of trailing them.

Yaris had not wasted any time, Rogan discovered. The tracks were widely spaced, indicating that the gang leader was suddenly in a hurry to be some place else. Rogan had no difficulty following at a fast clip, and shadows were beginning to slip into his surroundings by the time he found the spot where Yaris had camped for the night. He made camp at the same spot and boiled water for coffee before unrolling his bedroll. Night had settled by the time he turned in, and he was awake and ready to ride the next morning as soon as there was enough light to see tracks.

Rogan realized he was heading deeper into Indian Territory, and did not see another human as the day passed. Again he made camp on the spot Yaris had picked the day before, and was up and moving around before daybreak to be ready to continue trailing as soon as the sun showed. After the first two days the time seemed to pass unmeasured, and four more days rolled by in quick succession with no sign that the outlaws were nearing their objective.

He was now riding through broken country, and kept a close eye on his surroundings as he progressed. Even so, he was shocked when a voice suddenly called to him from cover on his left and he looked around to see a motionless rider only a few yards away covering him with a pistol.

'Hold up there, mister,' the man said sharply. 'Just sit still and get your hands up or you'll collect a slug.'

Rogan obeyed, lifting his hands shoulder high. The man gigged his mount forward and emerged from his cover.

'I heard you coming a long way off,' he declared. 'You're in an all-fired hurry, so what's your business?'

'I'm looking for someone,' Rogan replied.

'Yeah, I suspected that.' The man grinned. 'You sure had your eyes glued to those tracks. So who are you trailing and what's your business?'

'Are you a lawman?' Rogan ventured. The man laughed and shook his head.

'The hell I am! That breed don't live long out here, I can tell you. So who are you? And be quick with your answer.'

'I'm Buck Rogan. I ride for Al Spooner and I'm looking for Jake Yaris to give him some information about Spooner. I was at the Marlowe ranch several days ago. Marlowe said he was a friend of Yaris and showed me these tracks. He said they would lead to Yaris. Now perhaps you'll tell me who you are.'

'Steve Reddell. I ride with Yaris. We were at Marlowe's place half a week ago. I'm looking for sign of anyone following us. Yaris has a nose for that sort of thing and he had a hunch someone was on our trail so I dropped back to check for strangers, and you showed up. You better be who you say you are, Rogan, or you'll have a mighty lonely grave out here. Sit still while I remove your guns and then I'll take you to Yaris.'

Rogan remained motionless until he had been disarmed.

'OK.' Reddell nodded. 'Now keep following those tracks you were so interested in. Yaris is waiting at a small hideout near here while I check the area, and you better hope he'll believe your story because if he doesn't then time is running pretty short for you. Go on, get moving.'

Rogan took up his reins and continued. Reddell dropped back a couple of yards and kept a pistol in his hand. They went on in silence, and Rogan wondered at his sudden change of luck. After days of monotonous trailing he was actually being taken to Yaris. But he did not fool himself about the dangers attendant on this turn of events. Yaris would shoot him out of hand if he doubted the bluff Rogan was prepared to push.

After roughly two miles Rogan found himself entering a narrow defile which inclined into a wider gully. When he rode around a bend in the gully the vista opened out into a wide flat area. He saw a pool of water close to a steep rock wall. Six horses were tied to a picket line — one of them being the bay which belonged to Rogan — and he spotted the mouth of a cave higher up in the opposite rock wall with a well-defined path leading to it. Three men were seated around a small campfire, and the smell of cooking sharpened Rogan's senses, for he had been living on cold food for several days. There was also the aroma of coffee, which made him moisten his lips.

The trio around the fire scrambled to their feet and drew their pistols as Rogan rode towards them, but they relaxed somewhat when Reddell appeared at his back.

'Who you got there, Steve?' one of the three asked.

'I caught him following us! He reckons Spooner sent him, and Marlowe showed him our tracks at his spread and told him to follow them, so here he is. Where's Yaris?'

'In the cave. He's been waiting for you to get back. He's keen to get on to the big hideout.'

Reddell motioned with his drawn gun. Rogan walked to the path leading to the cave and began to ascend the steep incline, followed closely by Reddell. Halfway up to the gaping cave mouth Rogan trod on a loose rock which turned under his boot. He lost his balance, fell to his knees and then slid back down the slope. He tried desperately to recover his balance but failed, and his boots thudded against Reddell's legs, causing the man to topple over backwards. Reddell uttered a yell which was cut short as the back of his head came into violent contact with a rock.

Rogan rolled to the bottom of the slope before he stopped his plunge and lay motionless while his senses gyrated. He opened his eyes to find the three hardcases standing over him with drawn guns and suspicion on their hard faces. One of them turned to check the motionless Reddell.

'I slipped,' Rogan said as he got to his feet. He rubbed his right elbow, mindful of the guns pointing at him.

'And you knocked Steve over,' one of the men declared. 'Is he OK, Pete?'

'He's out cold, and it looks like he's busted his right leg,' Pete replied in a grim tone. 'Gimme a hand to get him over to the fire.'

The two hardcases holstered their guns and turned to Reddell. Rogan could not believe his change of luck as they lifted the unconscious badman and bore him over to the campfire. Rogan saw Reddell's discarded pistol on the ground and bent to pick it up. As his fingers closed around the butt he threw a quick glance up at the cave mouth but saw no sign of movement there. He turned instantly to cover the badmen.

Rogan cocked the pistol and moved forward. The trio were intent on the injured Reddell — had apparently accepted Rogan's story in the exigencies of the moment. Rogan covered them. They looked up at the sound of the metallic clicks of the .45 being cocked, and froze when they discovered they were looking into the black muzzle of the weapon.

'Stand up and get rid of your hardware,' Rogan ordered. 'One at a time, lift your guns and toss them behind you. Don't try anything or you'll be knocking on the door to Hell before you can blink.'

Disbelief showed on their hard faces as they arose and raised their hands. One by one they lifted their pistols from their holsters and tossed them back out of reach. Rogan glanced towards the cave but there was no sign of movement up there and he began to breathe more easily.

'Two of you, get down on your faces,' he ordered. 'Stick your hands up above your heads and don't even blink.' He waited until they had complied and then spoke to the third man. 'Get that rope over there and bind your sidekicks. Make it quick. Time is running out for all of us. Don't make a sound or I'll start shooting. You'll live through this if you do like you're told.'

The hardcase looked as if he wanted to protest but the menace of Rogan's gun forced him to obey. Rogan kept an eye on the cave mouth, fearing Yaris would appear. Time seemed to stand still while he waited for the hardcases to render themselves harmless.

'Tie them tightly,' he ordered. 'I'll check your knots when you've finished.'

When the two men were hogtied, Rogan motioned for the third man to get down. He moved in close as the man complied and struck him across the back of the head with the barrel of the pistol, rendering him unconscious. He worked quickly to tie the man, and then removed the discarded weapons to a safe distance. He checked on the unconscious Reddell, found him inert, and turned his attention to the cave.

He ascended the incline to the cave, pistol in his right hand, and sweat ran down his face. He estimated that Yaris and one other was in the cave, and steeled his nerve for action because Yaris had not looked like a man who would surrender to the law. He reached a flattened area just in front of the gaping cave mouth and eased in against the outside wall. There was no sound or movement from within the cave.

Rogan drew a deep breath and restrained it for a few moments to steady his racing pulses. His heart was pounding. He eased forward to enter the cave, but halted when he heard a voice which he recognized as belonging to Yaris. It echoed hollowly in the close confines of the gloomy cave.

'Trig, why in hell don't you go out there and see what's happened to the grub they're supposed to be cooking? And if Reddell is back then send him up here. I told him to take a quick look around and report back to me. I need to get back to the big hideout before we start out for Westville. Time is vital in this job, but nobody but me seems to be concerned. I'm beginning to think it's time we quit this business while we're still ahead. Those deputies Judge Parker is sending out from Fort Smith are sure making a nuisance of themselves now. Maybe we should move to Texas and set up business there, huh?'

'Times are changing, Jake,' Trig replied. 'I'll go shake them up about the grub although it ain't worth eating if Jack has cooked it.'

Rogan stepped back out of the cave mouth and flattened himself against the wall outside, pistol upraised in his right hand. He heard boots scuffing on solid rock, then saw a tall figure appearing from the gloom of the cave. The man emerged from the cave and paused at the entrance to look down at the campfire. He saw the three outlaws lying hogtied on the ground and jerked forward a fraction to peer more closely, as if unable to believe his eyes.

'What the hell?' he ejaculated, and as he halfturned to re-enter the cave his gaze fell upon the motionless Rogan. Shock filled his expression and his mouth opened.

Rogan was lunging forward even as the man turned, and the heavy barrel of his pistol crashed solidly against the side of the man's head. He grasped the man's shirtfront as he went down with a groan and eased him to the ground, pausing only to jerk a pistol from his holster. Straightening, Rogan prepared to enter the cave and confront Yaris, and at that moment a rifle cracked and a slug smacked against solid rock close to his head. He ducked as the bullet screamed away in ricochet, looked down towards the campfire and saw Reddell, lying on the ground, working a rifle and levelling it for a second shot. Rogan threw himself into the cover of the cave.

'What the hell is going on out there?' Yaris came forward from the gloom at the rear of the cave, his red beard bristling. He hesitated when he saw Rogan sprawled at the entrance and pulled up short when he realized that Rogan was a stranger. His right hand flashed to his hip for the pistol holstered there.

'Leave it be!' Rogan called, his voice echoing. 'I'm the law, Yaris, and you're under arrest.'

Yaris did not pause in drawing his weapon. The pistol cleared leather and swung up amazingly fast. Rogan had not expected the gang boss to surrender, and fired his deadly pistol an instant before Yaris could cover him. The blast of the shot was deafening in the close confines of the cave. Gun smoke flared. Yaris jerked upright under the impact of the bullet which struck him squarely in the centre of the chest. He stood erect for a moment, trying desperately to work his pistol, but the weapon spilled from his hand. His mouth gaped and blood suddenly dribbled from it. He groaned, twisted sharply, and dropped to the ground inertly as the gun echoes faded.

Rogan discovered that his teeth were clenched and tried to relax as he pushed himself to his feet, smoking gun ready. He went to where Yaris was lying and ascertained that the outlaw was dead. Then he turned to face the cave mouth. He eased forward until he could look down at the campfire, and exhaled his breath in a long sigh when he saw Reddell stretched out with the rifle discarded at his side.

It came to him then that his mission was over except for the minor details and he left the cave with relief slowly enveloping him.

He was aware that it would be a long, hard ride to Fort Smith with his prisoners, but he was looking forward to every step of the way.

THE END

We do hope that you have enjoyed reading this large print book.

Did you know that all of our titles are available for purchase?

We publish a wide range of high quality large print books including:
Romances, Mysteries, Classics
General Fiction
Non Fiction and Westerns

Special interest titles available in large print are:
The Little Oxford Dictionary
Music Book, Song Book
Hymn Book, Service Book

Also available from us courtesy of Oxford University Press:
Young Readers' Dictionary
(large print edition)
Young Readers' Thesaurus
(large print edition)

For further information or a free brochure, please contact us at:
Ulverscroft Large Print Books Ltd.,
The Green, Bradgate Road, Anstey,
Leicester, LE7 7FU, England.
Tel: (00 44) **0116 236 4325**
Fax: (00 44) **0116 234 0205**

Other titles in the
Linford Western Library:

RUNNING CROOKED

Corba Sunman

Despite his innocence, Taw Landry served five years in prison for robbery. Freed at last, his troubles seemed over, but when he reached the home range, they were just beginning. He was determined to discover who'd stolen twenty thousand dollars from the stage office in Cottonwood. But Taw's resolution was overtaken by events. Murder was committed and rustling was rife as Taw tried to unravel the five-year-old mystery. As the guns began to blaze — could he survive to the final showdown?

JUDGE PARKER'S LAWMEN

Elliot Conway

'Hanging' Judge Parker orders Marshal Houseman and his greenhorn deputy, Zeke Butler, to deal with raiders who are burning out Indian farmers in the Cherokee Strip in Indian Territory. Houseman begrudgingly sets off with Zeke, doubting he could be of any help at all. But with the aid of Bear Paw, and some of his kin, the two lawmen face the raiders in a series of shoot-outs, which prove Zeke to be one of the Judge's toughest manhunters.

DEAD MAN'S JOURNEY

Frank Roderus

The Civil War took everything from Alex Adamley. He was once the captain of the blockade runner the *Savannah Belle*. He'd been crippled; left penniless; his ship destroyed and his home and family gone. Yet his dead brother had left him some property in the distant West. Alex determined to go and see this property. He started walking ever westward . . . on a journey that would end in the toughest fight of his life. He was on a Dead Man's Journey.

A RECKONING AT ORPHAN CREEK

Terrell L. Bowers

When Sandy Wakefield, Flint's uncle, dies in a mining mishap, Flint and Johnny Wakefield suspect foul play. Sandy was trying to improve the miners' lot, who work long hours in dangerous conditions for a pittance. Then, Flint and Johnny discover the stripped body of an unknown man and seek to learn his identity. But life above ground gets as dangerous as below. Ultimately, it seems, Flint will have to die before there can be a reckoning at Orphan Creek!

RENEGADE GOLD

Robert Anderson

In Goldrush, an Indian uprising forces Kit Napier to rediscover his skills as an army scout. It wasn't the Indians who started the war, rather those white men plotting to supply them with guns for payment in gold. But their payment was destined to be made in blood. In partnership with a saloon girl, he fought both the renegade Indians and treacherous members of his own race: a desperate bid to prevent the territory going up in flames.

THE LONG CHASE

Alan Irwin

Jake Madison quit his job as marshal in Wildern, Wyoming Territory, when his wife Emma was killed during a bank raid by outlaw Bart Peary. Jake embarked on a hunt for the killer, which took him to Colorado, the Texas Panhandle, and the Indian Territory. Jake was facing a dangerous and difficult task, so even with the help of a retired army scout and two prospectors could he ever succeed in bringing Bart Peary and his associates to justice?